Harlequin

is pleased to announce the forthcoming release of its first motion picture, based on the best-selling novel by Anne Mather

---

Harlequin Presents...

KEIR DULLEA · SUSAN PENHALIGON

Leopard in the Snow

Guest Stars

KENNETH MORE · BILLIE WHITELAW

featuring GORDON THOMSON as MICHAEL
and JEREMY KEMP as BOLT

Produced by JOHN QUESTED and CHRIS HARROP
Screenplay by ANNE MATHER and JILL HYEM
Directed by GERRY O'HARA

An Anglo-Canadian Co-Production

OTHER
Harlequin Romances
by JANE ARBOR

CHAPTER ONE

'AUNT URSULA isn't entirely or quite our aunt,' explained Jason. 'Just a half-aunt, that's all.'

'So what?' challenged Lesley. 'It's only that Grandpa already had her when he married Grandma as his second wife, and they had Mother when Aunt Ursula was fifteen. Which makes her our aunt, even if she is only a half, doesn't it?' she appealed.

'Let's recap, may we?' suggested Dinah, seeking light. 'I agree with Lesley—she is your aunt. One doesn't distinguish aunts by halves. But I haven't met this one yet, have I?'

'Because she hasn't been to England since we moved here to Sherewater,' supplied Jason.

'And I *told* you,' reiterated his twin,' she married a madly rich Italian named Vidal, who is dead now, but Aunt Ursula still lives in Venice—in a palazzo on a canal—imagine!'

Dinah's nod acknowledged that, along with a welter of other information, she had already heard this. 'Yes, you did tell me,' she agreed. 'And she lives with her son—right?'

'Named Cesare. Our half-cousin. All right—cousin. But much older than we are. At least thirty or more,' said Lesley.

'And what makes you think you would be welcome on a visit to Venice?' pursued Dinah. 'Has your aunt

5

invited you, named a date, or what?'

The twins looked at each other, then both spoke together.

'Not exactly *invited*,' admitted Lesley.

'But we know she would love us to go,' claimed Jason. 'She's often said so in letters. And she always sends us Christmas presents and whopping money-orders for our birthday.'

'But you don't propose to descend on her—just like that?' Dinah queried.

Virtuous shock was registered in both teenage faces.

'Oh *no*,' said Jason. 'We've written to her to suggest our going, though we haven't posted the letter yet. We've explained, you see, that we must go now in the summer vacation, before Lesley goes into nursing, and I go to agricultural college. It's our only chance.'

'I believe Venice can be terribly hot and crowded in August, as I'm going to find,' Dinah warned.

'Yes, well—too bad. But we still want to go.'

'And what do your people say about it? Do they agree?'

'Oh yes, they're all for it. You know how they believe in Experience with a capital E. Which makes it all the more odd that Mother should suddenly come over all maternal and protective wings, flatly refusing to let us go the way we want to go. Considering how she's always encouraged all of us to do our own thing, it's quite out of character, this veto, wouldn't you say?'

To Dinah's knowledge of the Herbert family, it was. The twins' father was a dedicated research

6

chemist, their mother an artist of something more than talent. There were two children younger than the seventeen-year-old twins; all of them criticised by the narrow-minded as 'dragged up' and approved by the broad-minded as liberated'; the result to date appearing to be a mainly happy one, however achieved. And for Mrs Herbert to put a damper on any scheme of which she mainly approved did savour of the unexpected, Dinah agreed.

She said cautiously, 'I'd say it depends on how you propose to go. How do you?'

'Well, by car. Air-ferry to Le Touquet; drive across France; over the Alps and down to Venice that way. It would be an Adventure instead of just a journey. But the parents won't hear of it, even though I passed my driving test while I was still at school, and in a couple of months more I'll be able to vote,' Jason protested.

'Which hasn't much to do with your competence for driving across Europe. I don't wonder your mother won't hear of it,' Dinah commented.

There was a pause. Then Lesley said, 'Well, that's just it, you see. I mean, why we've come to see you. Because we thought—— Well, you are going to Venice yourself, aren't you? You have to go?'

'But not yet. I've got a month's leave before I take over from the clerk I'm replacing in the Venice office. And when I do go, I shall fly, paid for by the firm.'

'And you wouldn't, whatever happened, consider going earlier—say next week perhaps?' Lesley coaxed.

It wasn't difficult to guess what was coming. Dinah

7

said bluntly, 'You mean with you—*if* you were going to be allowed to go by car—which you're not?'

Jason took a turn. 'Ah, but we might. In fact, we're pretty sure we would be, if you were coming along. You're an experienced driver, and Mother trusts you. You'd still be on holiday when you got to Venice, and surely it would be much more fun spending it there instead of here? Besides, think—if you don't agree to come, we can't go either, so how will you like to have that on your conscience, h'm?'

Dinah dealt with this moral blackmail as it deserved. 'I've an idea my conscience would bear up,' she said. 'But——'

Both twins pounced on her hesitation. 'You'll think about it? You *might*?' they clamoured.

'Well——' Dinah shook her head. 'No promises until I've seen your people, *and* talked to my own. Anyway what about the return journey? I shan't be coming back, you know.'

Clearly this problem hadn't been considered. But they dismissed it with an airy, 'By that time we shall have done the trip one way and we shall know all the snags,' in favour of forcing from Dinah a decision on the present one—a cause in which they didn't succeed that day, owing to Dinah's insistence on learning and facing all the facts, and getting the blessing of all four parents on the project before she would give even a guarded agreement to it.

But the twins were nothing if not hustlers. They coaxed and cajoled, and showed sweet reason and compliance in all the right places, and, being granted permission to go ahead, had organised all their own and the secondhand Mini's papers with surprising efficiency and speed. With the result that, a week later, with three day's travelling behind them, they and Dinah and the car were committed to the arduous climb up to the Simplon Pass before they made the long drop down into Italy.

The twins' ruling consideration was economy, being determined to pay for the trip from their own savings and 'going Dutch' with Dinah on every expense the party incurred. If Dinah hadn't insisted that they all sleep at motels or inexpensive *relais routiers,* she thought they would have camped out each night, and now, on the slopes of the Alps, they had persuaded her to allow the car to bypass the Simplon Tunnel and the costly train, and to do the whole climb by road.

Dinah was driving. The Mini was finding the hairpin turns and sudden steep gradients hard going. Holding it to the road and continually changing gear took all her concentration until, after a glance at the instrument panel, she had to announce as casually as she could, 'This car is about to boil,' and pulled to a halt at the side of the narrow road.

Jason defended the car. 'She should have been game to take it.'

'To your knowledge, has she ever had to face an Alp before?' Dinah enquired drily.

'So now what?'

They all got out and gathered at the front of the car. 'Did you fill up the two-gallon plastic thing with

9

water this morning, before we left Lausanne?'
Dinah asked Jason.

He coloured. 'Help! I forgot. I checked the tyre-
pressures and—— Why, has she boiled away all
the water she had?'

Dinah waited to reply until a big car of international fame purred past them to the next bend fifty
yards ahead. Then she said, 'Probably, and thanks to
you, we haven't any.'

Better look, hadn't we?' Jason cocked his head,
listening. 'That car has stopped too. Same trouble
as ours, d'you suppose?' he asked on a misery-loves-
company note.

'Do you think it's likely, with a car of that quality?'
Dinah moved closer as Jason reached for the
radiator-cap, then leaped back, wringing his hand in
pain. 'Ouch! That's h——!'

He didn't finish, as a hand on his shoulder thrust
him back and another hand flung Dinah aside.

'You young fool!' the voice of the newcomer muttered thickly in English. 'You too,' he adjured Dinah.
'Hanging over the thing like that—asking to be
scalded and scarred for life! If he had got it open,
you'd have been sprayed with steam. Keep back. Let
it cool, and don't dare touch it until it does.'

He brushed off his hands, frowning at the three
of them, while they, recovering from shock, sur-
veyed him.

He was young, tall, dark. His glossy hair grew back
from an even line. Later in life, cut *en brosse*, it might
lend him distinction, but now it swept back towards
his nape in a single, youthful swath. His face was

narrow over thin bones; his eyes, behind sunglasses, were not visible; his hands, which had dispensed caution so roughly, were as spare of flesh as his face. He was dressed in the careless garb of his time— slacks and an open-necked shirt. But somehow he lent them elegance, and the shirt at least was of pure silk. All of a piece with that car, was Dinah's summing-up thought as she heard Lesley beginning to speak.

'You're English,' Lesley told the stranger.

He shook his head. 'No. Italian.' Now it was possible to discern a faint accent.

'Then how did you know we were English?'

'You are carrying GB plates, aren't you? I noticed them as I overtook, and came back to see if you were in trouble. Which it seems you were.' He turned to Jason. 'Carrying any spare water for when it cools down?'

' 'Fraid not.'

The young man's brows went up, making it possible to imagine the widening of his eyes. 'You set a car of this size—with three of you up—to the Alps up to the Pass, and you don't carry any water in case of overheating on the way? Who is driving the thing, anyway? Who is responsible?'

They might deserve it, but Dinah resented the scold in his tone. 'I was driving,' she said.

'And it's my car,' said Jason, sharing the blame.

'And you realise you passed the Tunnel station a long way back? Why didn't you take the train?'

'Because it costs money and we're travelling to a

11

budget. Are you carrying any water you could let us have?'

The question was ignored, as if it had no meaning for the big car's owner. He asked, 'At least you have a container? Oh, you have? Then you had better cut back—a quarter of a kilometre, no more. There's a spring gushing out on to the road. You can fill from it, and carry the water up. I'll wait and see you on your way before I leave.'

When Jason had left, running downhill, Dinal felt thanks were in order, and offered them. They were brushed carelessly aside. 'Where are you making for if you manage to get over the Pass?' the young man asked.

'Domodossola.' Dinah didn't mention Venice, lest she invite more sarcasm on the folly of their hoping to reach it.

He nodded. 'You should manage that tonight. Any other mishaps on your way?'

'None until now,' she told him, pleased she could say so. Very soon Jason came panting back and presently their knight-errant judged it safe to open up the radiator.

They piled into their seats, Jason driving now. They were shepherded by the big car, driven slowly behind them, to the top of the next sharp gradient. Then it accelerated and swept past. The driver sketched a farewell with a raised hand; Jason replied with a squawk of the Mini's horn, and then they were on their own once more.

Lesley, whose criterion was the latest glamorous

star on the pop scene, sighed, 'What a very dreamy young man!'

Jason grunted, 'How can you tell? Behind those glasses he's probably wall-eyed. And just how conceited can you get, owning a car like that?'

Dinah said nothing, fingering her wrist, which had been cruelly wrenched when she had been flung out of danger. She was blaming herself; she ought to have checked with Jason that they were carrying spare water—it had been foolhardy to expect the little car to negotiate these heights without overheating. Wiser still, she should have overruled the twins and insisted on their taking the train. Hindsight could see the folly of it all, but she wished she hadn't had to suffer its being pointed out so critically by that man. She had briefly felt the attraction of his easy, assured elegance and she would not have been feminine if she would not have liked praise from him, not blame.

Achieving the top of the Pass at last was a triumph. On the scree of the open plateau there were other cars and people, who had braved the climb. A colossal carved wooden eagle marked the six thousand feet of height above sea-level; there were St Bernard dogs —off duty at this season—in a big compound; the inevitable souvenir shop and the famous Hospice, lending part of itself as an international youth centre.

The panorama was a whole sky's width; the faraway peaks mistily blue where they weren't snowclad; the nearer ones green and comparatively gentle under scrub and young pines. '*Now* aren't you glad we didn't creep through on the train?' Jason demanded of the other two, and they were.

They made Domodossola by late dusk, found themselves a cheap hotel and were away again early in the morning, slipping down through the foothill border country to the plain of Lombardy. After Milan, Venice lay ahead; they reached it by evening, approaching it through an ugly industrial area by way of the wide causeway which brought them to the car's, if not their own, journey's end. Jason was disgruntled at having to abandon it on the huge parking-island at the point where all road and rail transport stopped as far as the city was concerned. Thereafter Venice's only highway was water.

They unloaded their packs from the car and presented, Dinah realised, a pretty grubby, laden and travel-worn trio. She suggested adjourning to the nearby railway station for a wash and brush-up, from which they emerged somewhat cleaner, though still burdened like packhorses. Over a cup of coffee they discussed plans.

A woman in the cloakroom had told Dinah they could either take a water-taxi or catch the cheaper *vaporetto* from the adjacent Piazzale Roma for the nearest landing-stage to the Palazzo d'Orio on the Grand Canal, the twins' aunt's address. As none of them knew what was the nearest landing-stage they needed, Dinah ruled they must take the taxi; she had seen some moored at the station entrance steps. She would deliver the twins into their aunt's care, then go herself to the hotel where she had provisionally booked a room, not having known just which day they might arrive.

'I suppose you did tell Signora Vidal that your

14

timing might be a bit elastic?' she questioned the twins casually.

'Oh yes,' they said in chorus.

'But you were able to give her some idea of when to expect you—today, tomorrow or whenever?'

This time they only nodded, and something furtive in their glances at each other made Dinah suspicious.

'Well, you did, didn't you?' she pressed.

No answer. Then Jason began, 'Yes, well, you see——' and Lesley continued, 'It's like this. Aunt Ursula doesn't know when to expect us, because *actually* she doesn't know yet that we're coming.'

Dinah stared. 'Doesn't know? But when you came to me, you'd already written to her, inviting yourselves! You told me——'

'That we'd written, not that we'd posted the letter then.'

'But you have posted it since—after I'd agreed to come with you, and you had your people's permission to come?'

'Oh yes—after that, but not soon after. In fact, not until the day before yesterday—wasn't it?' Lesley appealed to Jason. 'In Lausanne, missing the last post out. So we think Aunt Ursula can't know yet, unless Swiss and Italian mails are a lot faster than ours.'

'But why? How could you be so inconsiderate, so rude?' Dinah protested. 'You, Lesley, if not Jason, ought to know what having guests entails—extra meals, beds to be prepared, the lot.' But even as she spoke Dinah doubted whether in the Herbert haphazard household the extra mouth to be fed or the extra body to be bedded had ever caused much concern to the hosts. In Dinah's experience their friends and acquaintances and even near-strangers dropped in and left again equally unbidden. So it was with some doubt that Dinah questioned, 'Anyway, surely your mother at least would want to know her sister expected you?'

Again both twins looked sheepishly guilty. 'But we didn't lie,' Jason pointed out. 'We told her we'd written to Aunt Ursula, and we just let her assume it was all right. If she had asked, we should have had to tell her, of course, that we hadn't actually heard we should be welcome. But she didn't—she's so busy with this show of paintings she's sharing with someone, and Father has been attending a convention in York anyway, so *he* wasn't bothered.'

'And what was all the secrecy in aid of, may one ask?' urged Dinah.

'Well, just so that we couldn't be turned down, of course. After we'd set our hearts on coming, and had made all our plans, and enlisted you, we couldn't *bear* anyone to say, "Sorry, but it's not on, chaps." You *must* see that?' Jason appealed.

'And besides,' put in Lesley, 'we calculated that not knowing couldn't hurt Aunt Ursula too much. I don't suppose, being so rich, that she's ever made up a bed herself since she married, and she can't be so near the breadline that she would have to send out for a couple of extra hamburgers for our supper. Well, can she?' Lesley appealed in her turn.

Exasperated by what they saw as simple logic, Dinah practically ground her teeth at them. 'I could cheerfully beat you both,' she told them. 'You don't

16

deserve to be welcomed at an allotment hut, let alone a palace on Venice's Grand Canal. Besides, who's going to take the blame for apparently going along with it with you——? Old Muggins, that's who. In other words—me! Come on then. Let's go.'

Subdued, they followed her to the line of moto-*scafi*, where the boatman, with whom she bargained in his own language, nodded his knowledge of the Palazzo d'Orio and helped them all into his boat.

The time was evidently the evening rush-hour. The quays were alive with strolling tourists and hurrying workers; the water of the canal heaved and churned under the onslaught of dozens of motorboats, the occasional barge and the fussy water-buses, crowded to their handrails, which chugged up and down and across from one landing-station to the next. Most of the bordering buildings came sheer down to the water; their proprietor's private craft moored between drunken mooring-posts; their lower frontages still scarred by the marks of the high-water level of the tragic flood-tides of a few years earlier. By the time their boat turned into the wider stretches of the Grand Canal the twins' faces had begun to show their disillusionment with their surroundings.

'It's all a bit tatty, isn't it?' remarked Jason, eyeing blackened timbers and peeling shutters and rusty mooring-chains. 'D'you suppose any of it ever gets a coat of paint?'

Lesley said, 'There's supposed to be a Lido. I expected beaches and super hotels. Where are they?'

Dinah, who at least knew her Venice in theory, said, 'Not here. This is the city of Venice; the Lido is

17

an island, a water journey away.' Privately she too
was a little disappointed in the Venice they were seeing and hearing at canal-level, but lifting her eyes up
and away to the great sweep of the buildings along the
curve of the Canal, every roofline a cut-out pattern
against the vivid evening sky, she realised she was
looking at the Venice Canaletto had painted, and she
was enchanted; grateful too that her job should have
brought her here to work.

After about ten minutes' run the boatman crossed
the water against the main traffic stream and edged
skilfully in alongside a moored cabin-cruiser, all shin-
ing chromium and paintwork in contrast to the worn
and patchy apricot-coloured brickwork against which
it gently bobbed. There were a few steps up to the
narrow quay; the man took them at a bound,
announced, 'Il Palazzo d'Orio,' helped his passengers
out, hauled out their luggage, accepted his fare and
swept away in the boat he hadn't troubled to moor.

The narrow building rose sheer, its flat façade
broken only by scrolled-iron balconies at second and
third-floor shuttered windows. The expanse of brick
and the closed shutters gave it a blind look; on one
side it was attached to its neighbour, on the other a
narrow water-channel ran back to a connecting wall.
Jason, indicating the channel, said, 'The tradesmen's
entrance, d'you suppose? What a dump! This can't
be it, can it? Just look at the front door—it can't have
been opened in welcome for years!'

The door in question, magnificently carved and
flanked by two tall standard lanterns, was certainly a
formidable barrier. But as no more modest entrance

18

offered, Dinah used the kind of bell-pull which deserved an embroidered tassel, and was encouraged to hear it connect electrically within.

They waited, but not for long. The great door, which should have creaked and groaned, opened smoothly; the lanterns, springing to life, threw a faint path of light across the water before them, and behind the small crone in black who had opened the door, there was a glimpse of a marble-paved hall and some elegant furnishings.

The little old lady shook her head in answer to Dinah's inquiry for the Signora Vidal. 'The Signora is not here,' she said.

'She is out?'

'She is not here.' An expressive hand was waved outwards. 'She is away from home. Who wants her?'

Even the twins' lack of Italian got the message of that. Dinah heard them gasp. She said, 'The Signora's niece and nephew from England.'

'You, *signorina*?'

'No. I am just a friend.' Dinah thrust the twins forward. 'These two.'

'Ah, the Signora expects them? Knows that they come?'

'Well——' When Dinah hesitated, the crone nodded.

'Wait,' she said. 'Come in and wait. I shall fetch the Signore. He will know.'

The three stood in the hall, their baggage an untidy mound at their feet. When Lesley said, 'I suppose it was silly, our not posting that letter in time,' Dinah couldn't resist a sharp, 'Exactly. *Now* see where you've landed yourselves!' and Jason mused, 'The Signore. That'll be Aunt Ursula's son, our cousin Cesare. Well, thank goodness for him at least. Because if he has any cousinly feelings at all, he can't very well throw us out on the street.'

'If there *were* a street,' Lesley giggled nervously as a door down the hall was opened and a tall figure, escorted by the old lady as by a fussy tug, came down towards their group after dismissing her with a 'All right, Tomasa. I'll deal with it,' upon which she scuttled away.

Recognition was instant. The young man's glance, not hidden behind spectacles now, was not wall-eyed but dark, direct and critically questioning, summing up his visitors' nuisance value in much the same degree as his manner had seemed to measure it only as recently as yesterday afternoon.

'Well, well—fate working overtime to ensure that we should meet,' he remarked. 'But you gave me to understand that Domodossola was your objective, I thought?'

'Only for last night. We came on to Venice this morning, as we had planned,' Dinah told him.

'All the way from England in that carrycot of a car, and without troubling to announce yourselves until you arrived?'

'Not really. A letter was sent, but it must have been delayed,' Dinah lied gallantly for the twins' sake. 'You see, I'm afraid neither Jason nor Lesley envisaged that their aunt might not be here.'

'She is on holiday in America. She always leaves Venice to the tourists in August. I am Cesare, as you'll have guessed. You are Lesley?' He offered a hand. 'And Jason? And you are——?' he asked of Dinah.

'We're neighbours at home. My family and the Herberts are friends. I'm Dinah Fleming,' she said.

'Coming along for the ride, or in the role of chaperon?'

'Because Jason and Lesley asked me. Because their people didn't care for their coming alone, and because I was coming to Venice shortly in any case, to take up a job.'

'And meanwhile—your plans and theirs?'

Dinah looked at the twins, feeling it was time they laid their claim to a less chilly welcome than this. She herself hadn't anything to expect from the man, but the other two were his cousins, after all!

Evidently Jason read the hint in her glance. He said, 'Well, we hoped—— That is, we thought—— I mean, we expected Aunt Ursula to be here and that she would be glad to see us. It's an awfully long time since she last came to England, and we've never even seen *you*. And we did write, inviting ourselves—really! It's just that——'

'—Your letter went astray,' Cesare finished for him smoothly. He shrugged. 'Well, never let it be said we Venetians are wanting in hospitality. A moment.'

He went back down the hall and called Tomasa out from whatever dark recesses she had disappeared into. They talked in Italian. Dinah heard him order, 'Have the girls get the three third-floor rooms ready, and call in Giuseppe to take up the luggage. And they'll need dinner, I daresay. You'll see to that. No, not for me.' He turned back to the others. 'If you will go with Tomasa, I'll have your stuff sent up.'

Jason registered relief and muttered 'Thank you,' and Lesley echoed him. They waited for Dinah to go ahead of them. But she stayed where she was and they went with Tomasa without her.

She faced the surprise implicit in Cesare's raised eyebrows. 'Not for me, please,' she said. 'It's kind of you, but I'm not staying. I only came to see Jason and Lesley safe, and I've a hotel room booked in the city.'

'Where? At what hotel?'

'The Cavour.'

'I've never heard of it. It must be one of the tourist places.'

'It is. It's one of those at which we book in our clients.'

' "Your" clients?'

'My firm's clients. I work for Plenair, a travel agency, and I've come to join the Venice branch.'

'As?'

Dinah gave a small shrug. 'Maid of all work— clerk, courier, interpreter.'

'And you'll be living at this Cavour place?'

'Only temporarily, until I take over the apartment of the girl who will be going to the London branch in my place. But that won't be for a week or two yet.'

'So you are not committed permanently to the hotel, and can ring to cancel your booking, can't you?'

She stared, frowning. 'But I don't want to. I've told

22

you, I'm not staying. You don't have to put me up as well as your cousins!'

'And I'm telling you that, if you aren't willing to stay, after tonight they aren't staying either. Well?'

'But that's absurd,' Dinah protested. 'You can't turn them out. They came expecting a welcome from your mother, and their people will expect to hear of them in your care if they can't be in hers.'

'I could tell them, "Nice to have met you," and pack them safely back home.'

She could almost have stamped her foot at the airiness of the man's tone. 'You wouldn't dare!' she defied him. 'They're spending all their own money on this trip, and they are *not* being sent home.'

'Then I'll park them out with a dowager of my acquaintance. I know just the one who would take them for a fee. But be responsible for them here, I will not.'

'Why not?'

'Because I am a busy man; such leisure as I am able to earn I spend as I please, and I've no intention of playing sole guide and social entertainer to a couple of naïve teenagers who've been wished on me unbidden. Do I make myself clear?'

Dinah nodded. 'Perfectly. Clear too that you also make yourself sound incredibly selfish, and rather as if you spend any leisure you get in one long debauch for which you don't want witnesses!'

She expected a searingly sharp retort to the rudeness of that, and was a little taken aback when it did not come. He said coolly, 'I'd have put it rather less crudely myself, but as long as you get the message

23

that my pleasures are mainly adult, what's in a word? Meanwhile, I'm afraid my ultimatum stands—as I've no intention of recalling my mother from her holiday to take up her auntly duties to these youngsters. And as you aided and abetted their coming, while they want to stay in Venice the three of you will stay here; if you won't,. neither of them does. So please make up your mind.'

CHAPTER TWO

DINAH saw that she had no choice. But she said stiffly, 'I think you are being quite unreasonable about this. Jason and Lesley have both left school, and they are quite capable of looking after themselves, without any hindrance to you.'

'How old are they?'

'Seventeen.'

'And you yourself?'

'Twenty-four.'

'And having shepherded them so far, why abandon them now?'

'I suppose, because all I expected to have to do for them was to see them safely here.'

'But if, as you say, you have still some free time of your own, why not carry on the good work—"do" Venice as all good tourists do; mount the Campanile for the view, tour the Doges' Palace, eat ices on the Piazza and get yourselves serenaded by a gondolier in a ribboned hat? They'll love you for it, if that's what they came to Venice for.'

Dinah said, 'I rather think they came more for the Lido than for anything else, but that remains to be seen. Meanwhile, that's the second time you've used "tourist" as if it were almost a dirty word. Why?'

He shrugged. 'Call it prejudice. But Venice is and

always was a merchant city before the tourists took it over and pitied it—"Poor Venice—*so* shabby, but one feels one ought to see it before it sinks into the sea".'

His mimicry was so true of remarks which Dinah had heard often before that she softened a little towards him, and she said less testily, 'All the same, I suppose we're all tourists at some time or another. Or, when you go abroad yourself, do you think of other people "*They* are tourists, but *I* am a traveller"?'

For a moment a smile crooked the corner of his mobile mouth. 'I plead guilty,' he said. 'The Greeks had a word for it—*hubris*, they called it—snob pride. And doesn't everyone think of themselves like that? Don't you?'

Dinah shook her head. 'I don't know about everyone, but I don't think I do. And aren't you forgetting that tourism is my business?'

'Ah, yes.' He studied her for a long moment. 'A career woman at twenty-four.'

'I shan't always be tweny-four,' she pointed out.

'No, and in less than no time you won't be a career woman either. For don't tell me that in coming to work in Venice you hadn't at least one eye on possible Romance?'

'With an Italian? I don't think so.'

'Why not with an Italian? They come in as many shapes and sizes and attractions as Englishmen do— more, if you believe the song-writers.' He broke off to beckon to Tomasa who was hovering down the hall 'Giuseppe took up the *signorina*'s bags with the others, so please show her the way to her room now.' To Dinah he said, 'I'm dining out myself, so we shan't meet again this evening. Tomorrow you must tell me your plans for my cousins, and as far as possible the household shall co-operate.'

Practically spelling out that he regards me as their governess, thought Dinah as she followed the housekeeper up the stairs. As soon as they heard her coming the twins surged from their own rooms and into hers, eager with questions and criticisms of their host.

'Why did you stay behind? What has he been saying to you? Of all the things—his turning out to be the same chap who nagged us about going over the Pass! Didn't seem over-pleased to see us again, did he? Or even once, come to that. After he had got rid of us, what did he say?'

'He wouldn't hear of my leaving you to his tender mercies; said he couldn't undertake to entertain you. So I've agreed to stay on here for the time being,' Dinah told them. She looked round the room, at its marble floor, its thick-pile rugs, its carved furniture and canopied bed. 'Are your rooms as grand as this?' she asked.

'Just,' said Lesley. 'And there's a bathroom for the three of us to share. Funny, isn't it?—it's not a bit of the awful dump it looks from the outside. Almost grand, as you say.'

Dinah did not reply. She had gone to open the shutters beyond the tall window and found she could step out on to one of the small balconies they had noticed as they had arrived. The twins crowded behind her and they looked out on a breathtaking scene.

It was past dusk now; all the craft on the Canal were lighted, the water ink-dark, except where the lamps on the quays and the house-lamps threw shimmering paths of light across it. There was still noise, but up here it was muted. The buildings to left and right of the Palazzo d'Orio and across from it were now only dark silhouettes against the sky, where a single star hung in defiant competition with the man-made lights below.

'Poor Venice' indeed! Thought Dinah as she reluctantly closed the shutters at last and came back into the room. How dared anyone pity it or call it shabby? She found she was wondering who, and how many people, had said so to Cesare Vidal and how they had reacted to the caustic lash of his tongue in contradiction.

Lesley went to sit on the bed, watching as Dinah began to unpack and put her things away. Watching her own reflection in the long wardrobe mirror, Lesley mused wistfully, 'Do you suppose I'll ever lose my puppy fat and get as slim as you?'

Dinah straightened and looked into the mirror; saw the contrast between them—Lesley, round-limbed and rosy, straw-fair and long-haired; she, much slighter in build, grey-eyed under straight dark brows, glossy dark hair framing her face in two wings and turning inward in a pageboy-cut at her jawline. She consoled the younger girl, 'You'll thin down a bit, I daresay. But we're different shapes to begin with. You'd look wrong if you were skinny,

28

and anyway. I've always heard that Italian boys prefer blondes. We brunettes are two a penny around here.'

From where he lay stretched on the bed, hands behind his head, Jason interposed, 'What about Italian girls? And how does one communicate, if one hasn't a word of the lingo?'

Dinah laughed. 'If you're interested enough, I daresay you'll manage. It's been done before in dumbshow and will be again. And now, if you'll both make yourselves scarce, I'm going to get out of this gear and into something else before we eat.'

The clear light of a Venetian morning had them all up early. Cesare did not join them for the coffee and rolls which they took in a small room off the hall, but he appeared when they were poring together over a map of the city which Dinah had brought with her.

Overnight he had left a message with Tomasa for Dinah, saying that he had himself telephoned the Cavour that she would not be taking up her reservation, and when she thanked him he said carelessly, 'Just making sure of your keeping our bargain,' and went on to ask how they meant to occupy the day.

As Dinah had foreseen, the twins wanted to explore the Lido. As far as they were concerned, cultural and historic Venice could wait until they had sucked that particular orange dry. Could they get to the Lido by car, they wanted to know, and learned that they could, by car-ferry, or go by *vaporetto* from the Public Gardens.

'Which would be cheaper?' they asked.

'The steamer—only a few hundred lire.' Cesare turned to Dinah. 'You'll be going with us?'

But a perverse quirk of her will rebelled. She had claimed to him that the twins were capable of taking care of themselves, and this was the time to bear that out.

'I hadn't meant to,' she said. 'I'll go over sometime not today. I thought that instead I'd like to look in at the office of Plenair—to see where I'll be working, and to let the manager know I've arrived before time.'

Cesare frowned. 'There's time enough for that, surely?'

The frown annoyed her. She dug in her heels. 'That's what I'm doing this morning, anyway.'

'In that case I'll send Jason and Lesley in the boat with Giuseppe. I shan't be needing it this morning, and he can see them safely to the Lido and arrange a time to meet them for coming back.'

'Is that your craft that we saw at your front door?' asked Jason.

Cesare nodded. 'The same.'

'It's pretty super. Do you have to use it as you would a car, and is Giuseppe sort of your chauffeur?'

'And houseman and general factotum. I usually pilot the boat myself, but I can walk where I want to go today. So whenever you are ready to leave, Giuseppe will take you and see you safe. Will you be coming back for luncheon?'

'Need we, if we like it over there?'

'Not necessarily, if you let Tomasa know.'

'Then I guess we won't. Eh?' Jason consulted his

twin as they left the room together.

'And you?' Cesare asked Dinah when they had gone. 'Do you know the whereabouts of this office of yours?'

'Yes, it's on the Calle San Gallo off the Piazza San Marco. I've found it on the map, and it looks as if I can walk there from here.'

'Easily. It happens to be on my own way, and I'll walk with you. Incidentally,' he selected a letter from the small pile in his hand, 'this came this morning, addressed to my mother. I've opened it as you see.'

She took it, saw its Lausanne postmark and read it as he watched her.

'You see? Neither delayed nor sent astray—just posted a shade belatedly, don't you think?' he insinuated smoothly.

She nodded Yes.

'Even if my mother had been here, it was posted too late to warn her of an influx of guests who were almost bound to arrive before it. By whose design was that, one wonders?'

If he had believed the twins were to blame he would surely have tackled them about it. But no, he had to imply that she had engineered it! Deciding that for once Jason and Lesley could bear the brunt, she said, 'I'd understood that it had been sent much earlier. It was only after we had actually reached Venice that I learned we'd be making a surprise descent on you; that you had been advised far too late.'

'You didn't mention as much last night.'

'No Because, though I had scolded, I did understand a little why they had done it. They wanted so

31

very badly to come, so they had banked on their arrival being such a *fait accompli* that they couldn't possibly be turned down once they were here.'

'They little know how nearly they were,' he remarked.

She looked at him curiously. 'You really mean that if I hadn't agreed to stay, you wouldn't have entertained them?'

'Judge for yourself. I thought I'd made myself entirely clear on that,' he said.

He was waiting for her in the hall when she was ready to go out. She had traced her route on the map and she hoped he would take her by way of the quays and the great Piazza of San Marco. But a short distance from the house he turned back along narrow alleys and waterways and humped bridges, giving her her first view of the Venice of the back streets, a maze which she felt would take her months to explore.

She asked him what his own objective was, and he told her his bank, on the Riva del Carbon, not far from the Rialto Bridge.

'If you hadn't lent your boat to the twins, would you have used it to get to your bank this morning?' she asked.

'Probably. Within the city our craft has to serve as our car. Why?'

'Because I'm wondering why you inconvenienced yourself by letting them have it, when you had told them of two other ways they could get out to the Lido?'

Without looking up at him she was aware of the

slanted glance of his dark eyes. 'Perhaps,' he said, 'it was because I can recognise a petty reaction when I hear one.'

She worked that out. She didn't care for the result. 'You considered I was being petty for refusing to go with them?'

'Well, weren't you? Wasn't it your retort—the first you had been able to make—to my insistence that you assume responsibility for them while they are here?' he asked.

He was so uncomfortably near the truth that she flushed, and her defensive, 'I thought they could well be left to go by themselves and didn't need me along,' sounded weak even in her own ears.

'All the same, your prime motive was pique, and I think you know it. And as I can be petty too, that was why I sent Giuseppe with them as escort.' He paused. 'Is your question answered to your satisfaction?'

'I realise you feel you've answered it to *yours*,' she said with a new show of spirit, and was slightly disconcerted when he laughed.

'In other words, you're conceding victory. Which is just as well, for you may find by experience that I do like to win.'

Dinah made no reply to what she read as the consummate conceit of that, and the next remark came from him.

'Do you know any of your colleagues-to-be at Plenair?' he asked.

'Not the manager, who is Italian. The assistant manager is English; I've worked with him in the

London office, and I've spoken on the telephone to the Italian girl with whom I'm being exchanged,' Dinah told him.

'Are you fluent in Italian?'

'Fairly, I think. I spoke it first with an aunt who was Italian, and I've kept it up at night-school and in some crash courses.'

'And how long are you likely to be here?'

'Initially, until the end of the autumn. After that, I may be sent back to London, or I may stay on.'

They had turned into the Calle S. Gallo, and the long façade of the travel office was just across the street. Cesare saw her to the door and left her, and she went through into the wide foyer which was crowded with people; queueing at the *bureau de change*, inquiring at counters about local tours, being shepherded by couriers, using the foyer as a meeting-place with their friends.

Dinah, wanting to see before she was seen, was glad of the cover they afforded. She had told Cesare she wanted to make herself known to the manager, but wherever he was, he was not her objective just now. That was a private one, a curiosity of her own to gauge the effect upon her of the renewed sight of a man she knew would be here.

Trevor Land, with whom she had 'worked in the London office'—and who had now been promoted as assistant manager of the Venice branch six months previously. Trevor, earnest, conscientious Trevor; his promotion from senior clerk to a minor assistant managership his first step on the executive ladder he meant to climb. Trevor, dedicated. Trevor, as predictable as sun-up in such off-duty wooing of Dinah as he had allowed himself. Trevor, with whom she had been corresponding in 'Dear Trevor' and 'Dear Dinah' terms at intervals of about a month. Trevor, whose favourite conversation was 'shop'. Trevor, even rather . . . dull in comparison with—well, with whom in particular? Anyone special she knew?

She saw him now. She remembered his bland, open face, but she had almost forgotten how sturdily bulked he was and how short. He was standing behind a side desk, telephoning. Beside him at a typewriter sat a girl clerk, hands idle in her lap, as if she were awaiting the result of his talk, and something in the way she was looking up at him struck Dinah with a memory.

It was of herself, a little awed, a little worshipful of her chief, as Trevor had been for a time. The awe and the hero-worship hadn't lasted beyond her own advancement in her job. But mild intimacy had taken place; they had enjoyed off-duty hours together, and she was surprised to find she was questioning now that, as a man-to-woman relationship, it was satisfactory. Certainly it wasn't exciting, but how much excitement should one need?

He had replaced the receiver and was now talking to the girl. She was petite and pretty and looked over-eager to please. She was winding paper into her machine as Dinah moved forward and Trevor saw her.

She met his surprise with a smile, and while she explained her early arrival in Venice she was aware that the girl was not typing. She was listening, though Trevor and Dinah were speaking in English.

The manager, Signor Corotti, was on vacation, Dinah learned. Trevor was deputising for him and recounted in detail the extra duties this entailed. He introduced the girl as Etta Megio, his secretary, sketched for Dinah her probable work when she took it up, and summoned to meet her the girl with whom she was to exchange.

The two made an appointment for Dinah to see the apartment before she moved in, and it was only when these matters had been dealt with that Trevor suggested a rendezvous for luncheon.

'We close from noon until three-thirty, though I usually like to be back myself before then,' he said. 'I could meet you anywhere you like, or you could come back here at twelve to collect me.'

Inferring from this that she was not welcome to linger now, Dinah said she would go exploring in the meantime, and would come back. She was about to turn away when Etta Megio began to speak in rapid Italian, and that she was making a protest confirmed when he told Dinah,

'Etta is reminding me that we had arranged to lunch together today. But it was only in order for me to brief her on a project we have coming up, and it can wait until tomorrow.'

Dinah smiled at Etta, only to notice and to pity the girl's quivering chin and downcast eyes. Dinah said in Italian, 'And so could I wait until tomorrow —or any other day.' But Trevor would have none of that, and Etta did not look up.

Dinah came out on to the Piazza San Marco in

full sunshine. There were the milling people and the pigeons and the arcades and the open-air orchestras and the towering Campanile and the magnificent façade of the Basilica, just as she had heard them described, as she had seen them in paintings and as her imagination had pictured them—and she was grateful for the turn in her career which had brought her here.

It was all very well, she thought, for Cesare Vidal to belittle the tourists. *He* might be the son of his merchant city, but why shouldn't he expect to share its beauty with people who had to travel to it to see it? She reminded herself to point this out if the subject came up again. Let him win on that dog-in-the-manger attitude if he could!

Not looking forward very much to her date with Trevor, she filled in the intervening time with a window-gazing tour of the rich shops under the arcades. She was a little late and Trevor was waiting for her outside the closed doors of Plenair. He took her to a restaurant on a side quay, where they sat at a pavement table, facing a narrow canal.

'It's not exactly the Gritti Palace or the Royal Danieli,' he excused it. 'But the service is quick and it's handy for the office. You'll probably find it convenient to eat here too when you start work.'

Work. To Trevor the word was an elixir, a talisman, and it was not until he had outlined the project which he had intended to discuss with Etta that he asked Dinah to explain how and why she had come over so early.

She told her story once more and saw him frown

at the name of her own and the twins' host.

'Vidal?' he echoed. '*Vidal?* The three of you are staying with him? Yes, I know you mentioned him before, but in the office my mind was on other things, and the name didn't penetrate then.'

'Should it have done?' Dinah asked. 'Do you know him?'

'Know him?' Trevor used an expert fork on *spaghetti bolognese.* 'Everyone in Venice knows Cesare Vidal—knows *of* him at the very least.'

'As what?' Dinah inquired.

'For what he is—moneyed as Croesus; interests in everything from banking to silk and boat-building to glass, and still manages a playboy role on the side, with successive amours which are meat and drink to the gossip writers. A typical Italian—doing everything at speed, including conquering and discarding women. Vidal's latest acquisition, one hears, is the Principessa Lagna. They'll be seen everywhere together while it lasts, though as this one is Italian, he may be considering marriage to her.'

'Because she is a princess?' asked Dinah drily.

Trevor shook his head. 'Not that. Titles cut no ice in this country nowadays—they're only courtesy handles. No, I meant that though their men leap into and out of affairs with foreign women, they seem to end up by marrying Italians.'

'Cesare Vidal isn't wholly Italian. His mother is English,' Dinah pointed out. 'And aren't you generalising rather a lot? All Italian men can't be the fast movers in business and with women that you seem to claim.'

'Have it your own way. I speak as I find, and you did ask me what I knew of Vidal, and I've told you his reputation as all Venice knows it,' Trevor said stiffly.

'Perhaps I didn't expect it to be quite so colourful —tycoon, philanderer, the "constant companion" of princesses,' Dinah murmured, thinking that she understood now what Cesare meant by his adult pleasures, though she didn't say so aloud.

Trevor said, 'Yes, well, there it is. The man is a legend, no less.' He paused. 'I suppose it's a good thing you are too level-headed to fall for his type. But if he did try anything on, you'd be on your guard, wouldn't you?'

'I wouldn't compete with a princess, if that's what you mean,' said Dinah.

Trevor considered that. 'I don't know that it was, really,' he said. 'I know that you wouldn't throw yourself at *him*, but supposing he made a pass at *you*?'

'Over which neither of us need lose any sleep,' Dinah assured him. 'To Cesare Vidal I'm a shepherdess of teenagers, and he means to keep me nose-down to my duties.'

'And of course you won't be staying at the Palazzo d'Orio after the youngsters go home?'

'Of course not. I'm moving into Signorina Pacelli's apartment, aren't I? You know that.'

They lingered over their coffee until Trevor looked at his watch and said he would like to get back to the office. 'We must get together again before you start work. I'll ring you, and perhaps you would come to

39

dinner at my place one night? My landlady is a good cook.'

Which was the nearest Trevor would ever get to an invitation to go up and see his etchings, Dinah thought, amused. She told him she would like that, and on parting from him, said, 'I was sorry to cut in on your date with your secretary. Tell her so, will you, and take her out to lunch tomorrow—somewhere rather special?'

Trevor looked blank. 'I told you—I always lunch here,' he said.

The twins did not return until late afternoon, after Dinah had rested and taken a bath and changed into cream slacks and shirt. They were both lobster-red with sunburn, but clamoured that they had had a marvellous time; the Lido was fabulous, '*much* smarter than this part,' the shops and the hotels were out of this world, and the beaches fantastic, though whole stretches were private, only to be trespassed upon at a cost.

'You must go over with us tomorrow,' Lesley told Dinah. 'We had ices at the next table to an English couple, and they said you could find yourself sitting next to a film star or an Arab prince any time, the place is so swarming with celebrities, season after season. Do you suppose Cesare knows any famous people he could introduce us to? Have you seen any more of him today?'

'Not after he walked me to the office this morning. I had luncheon with Trevor Land—you remember, you've met him once or twice at home—and

40

then I came back here. Incidentally, if we do go to the Lido tomorrow, we aren't borrowing your cousin's launch again. He needs it for getting around himself,' said Dinah.

'Do we know what he does?' asked Jason idly. 'Does he work at anything, or is he just a man about town?'

'Trevor knows him and says he has business interests in all sorts of things.' Without enlarging on Trevor's further view of Cesare's reputation Dinah changed the subject to ask whether they didn't think they owed it to their Aunt Ursula to write to tell her of their unheralded descent upon the Palazzo d'Orio and of Cesare's acceptance of them in her absence.

They agreed it would be polite. 'But we don't know where she is.'

'Cesare will give you her address.'

'And we shall have to lie a bit, if we tell her he was glad to see us.'

'Then lie with your fingers crossed,' Dinah advised. 'At least he didn't throw you out.'

They dined alone again that night. Afterwards they experimented with television, but only succeeded in getting a dubbed American thriller which none of them wanted to see. Then Jason wondered aloud what free entertainment Venice's nightlife had to offer, and Dinah suggested a walk along the front of the lagoon and an ice or a drink on the Piazza San Marco, for which she would stand treat.

The night sky was dark velvet and the subtropical air a caress. 'Sensible folk, these Latins,' Jason approved the strolling, laughing, gossiping crowds. 'Take up to three hours for a snooze at midday, and then stay awake and enjoy themselves all night.'

Certainly the evening of the ordinary weekday might have been a gala occasion; gay with lights and street-music, the waterways still busy, the restaurants and hotels with welcoming open doors, and though the luxury shops were closed their windows were still ablaze with the temptation of expensive leather and crystal and lace and antiques. Moving with the crowd at its own pace, the three were content to pause when it paused—a fairly frequent occurrence when there was a press of people crossing its path or coming from the other way.

This was to happen at one of the principal landing-stages on the front, opposite to the mellowed red façade of the world-famous Royal Danieli Hotel, where there was mooring for private craft adjacent to the waterbus stage. A bus had pulled in, juddering at the stage, the passengers were jostling off, a group of them impeding the way of a couple who had come up the steps from the mooring basin.

The couple had halted. The man was Cesare. His hand was under the elbow of his companion, a silvery blonde in a metallic lavender evening gown, who was pressing closely to his side in intimate appeal for protection from the crowd. Jason chanted softly, 'Ho-ho—Cesare on the tiles! Who is his lady, d'you suppose?' while Lesley's louder pipe of, 'There's Cesare! Hi—Cesare!' caught his attention.

He looked their way, spoke briefly to the woman and thrust towards the three. He introduced them:

'My young cousins from England—Jason, Lesley, and their friend Dinah Fleming; the Principessa Lagna,' offering the lesser breed to the superior, as etiquette bade.

The princess drew her fringed lace shawl more closely about her shoulders before she gave her hand to the three in turn.

'Ah, the young cousins who arrive—so?' she said in English, and looked up at Cesare with extravagantly lashed and shadowed eyes. 'And already you allow them out on the streets—so late and unescorted?' she scolded playfully.

He laughed. 'Ah, but I've contracted out, from responsibility. I'm not in charge, Dinah is.' He addressed Dinah directly: 'What are you doing anyway? Where are you bound?'

'Nowhere in particular,' she told him. 'We came out for a walk, to see Venice at night.' At a slightly shocked sound from the Princess she added, 'After all, there are three of us, and on holiday in England in a strange place we'd do just the same—explore.'

'And it's true, you know, Francia,' Cesare said. 'Haven't I always told you that you Sicilians have an exaggerated view of the proprieties? Even here in the North——'

'Ah, here in the North you assail us just as often as you think you dare, and do not like it at all when you burn your fingers on our virtue—h'm?' She teased him archly.

He laughed again. 'And should we be men if we did not try?' he teased back. 'As for the English, they have an in-built rectitude. You heard Dinah

43

just now—they see no evil, so no evil befalls them. It is as simple as that.' He spoke to Dinah again. 'And where now?' he asked.

'We thought we'd have ices on the Piazza before we go back.'

'And Cesare'—the princess tucked a hand into the crook of his arm—'we must go too. The Lanellis will be waiting.'

'Yes.' He lifted a hand, the Princess smiled in gracious farewell, and the others watched until they disappeared through the main doors of the hotel.

Lesley spoke first. 'Do you know,' she said, 'I feel exactly as if I'd queued for hours to see the Queen attend a Command Performance, and she'd deigned to speak to me as she passed by?'

'Except that the Queen wouldn't have been so stuffy about our being out on our own. At our age —the nerve of the woman!' Jason scoffed.

'At least your cousin didn't agree with her. He seemed to see nothing wrong in our wanting to explore,' said Dinah. Privately she was thinking how completely in character Cesare had acted. He had shifted the load of responsibility on to her own shoulders and he had no intention of taking it back. Perhaps she should have been flattered, but illogically she wasn't. Just then she would gladly have exchanged his airy confidence in her for a little old-fashioned male concern. Merely a trace—was all she asked—of the kind of solicitude his look and touch showed for his Princess Francia Lagna.

A passing madness to expect it, of course. But she was envious of it, all the same.

CHAPTER THREE

The next day Dinah went to the Lido with the twins. They went by the *vaporette* and spent the whole day on the beach, sunbathing and swimming. After that they divided their time between going over there, sightseeing in the city and picking up the Mini from its park and driving out to explore the countryside.

Jason and Lesley went oftener to the Lido than Dinah did. As she had prophesied, by some chemical attraction which dispensed with language they had made friends with the two teenage boys and a girl of a Roman family who had taken a villa for the summer, and their financial affairs had been boosted by a lavishly generous money order from their aunt in answer to their letter to her which Dinah had advised.

Cesare was there when they opened the letter and passed the cheque over to him to cash for them. 'What does Mother say?' he asked.

Jason looked up. 'Oh, she's being super about our coming; says Welcome and all that; wishes she'd been here, but that we're to ask you for anything we—— Here, read it for yourself. There are a couple of pages. I haven't read it all yet.'

Cesare took the proffered sheets, read, and handed them back. 'You didn't get as far as the postscript?'

'No. What does it say?' Jason turned to the last page and read aloud:

'I like all you say, darlings, about your friend Dinah, without whose help you couldn't have got to Venice. She sounds a honey. Please thank her for me. And if she is as nice as you claim, remind Cesare of what happened to your Uncle Claudio in much the same boat, and tell Cesare Beware! *Arrivederci*, babes. All my love.'

There was silence in the room. Dinah, who was writing a letter home, bent more closely over it. Then Lesley puzzled, 'Why, what did happen to Uncle Claudio? What does Aunt Ursula mean?'

'By her warning to me? asked Cesare. 'You must have heard that my mother came to Italy as an *au pair* in my father's family, and that my father Claudio, the son of the house, fell in love with her and married her? Work it out.'

'But what's that got to do with———?'

'Oh, dimwit!' Jason struck in impatiently. 'Aunt Ursula is telling Cesare to beware of falling for Dinah, as Uncle Claudio fell for *her*. Both of them English girls, don't you see? But just a joke, mutton-head. J.O.K.E.—joke. Get it?'

'Oh,' said Lesley blankly. 'Oh, I see.'

'*No?*' her brother marvelled. 'Go to the top of the class. Meanwhile, are you coming out now? Dinah, what about you?'

But Dinah declined. 'I want to finish this letter before I keep an appointment at the flat of the girl I'm going to exchange with. In the lunch hour'— she looked at her watch—'I've got to walk over there, and it's nearly twelve now.'

'O.K. See you.' Dinah expected Cesare to go too, but he stayed. Unable to go on writing under his eye, she doodled idly until he said, 'You're wondering, aren't you, why I let Jason read my mother's post-script aloud?'

'Of course,' she said crisply. 'Why did you?'

'Perhaps because I thought it a pity you shouldn't hear how appreciated you were, even at secondhand report.'

'And perhaps not,' she disagreed. 'Sooner or later I'd have been shown the letter to read for myself, and I could have laughed off your mother's joke in private.'

'Then say, perhaps, I hoped to see you flattered by her conclusion that your charm was going to be a menace to my heart?'

He was laughing at her and that irked her. 'I don't think so,' she said. 'You must know Signora Vidal only meant what she said as a joke. Jason did at once, and so did I. But all the same, it embarrassed me, as you must have known it would.'

'And supposing *madre mia* wasn't joking?'

'Then all I can say is that you must have given her cause to think you're hopelessly susceptible, or she sees danger where none threatens—as we both know none does.'

He threw back his head with a shout of laughter, then said mock-gravely, 'Do you know what? This very day I'm going to cable to Mother, "Not to worry, Mother dear. Charm you may have been led to believe the lady has, but she also has an edge to

47

her tongue which is calculated to turn any man off."
How about that?'

'It sounds like a very expensive cable, and quite
unnecessary, I'd say.'

'Then you think she may be left to her illusions of
my danger?'

'If she ever had any, which I doubt. She wrote as
she did for a joke, as you must very well know.'

'If you say so. But we aren't quarrelling about it?'

'About anything so trivial? Of course not.' Dinah
looked at her watch again, stood up and collected
her writing things.

'Where is this apartment you are going to see?'
Cesare asked.

'On the Calle Maser.'

'Then you needn't walk. I can take you within a
stone's throw of it by launch. Are you ready to go
now?'

She wanted to tell him not to trouble. But it
would have been churlish to refuse, so she joined
him on the quay a few minutes later.

He turned off the main stream of the Grand Canal
into the Rio dei Barcaioli and again into a narrow
cut which he said led directly to the Calle Maser. He
moored the launch and seemed to expect to see
Dinah all the way to the house she wanted.

The street was deep in shadow, the tall shabby
buildings shutting out the sun. Some of the houses
looked empty behind their closed shutters; some
were numbered, some were not. Search brought
Cesare and Dinah eventually through a narrow
alley on to a small paved court where several lines

48

of domestic washing hung overhead. The house in question was the corner one of a block, Signorina Pacelli's flat the one on the top storey of four.

Cesare looked about him in distaste. 'You can't live here,' he said.

'It may be better inside. Anyway, I've promised to take over the flat,' said Dinah as they went through the open doorway and began to mount the stairs. Feeling more depressed than she cared to show, at that moment she was quite glad of Cesare's company.

Signorina Pacelli answered their ring and showed them into a tiny vestibule and a living-room for which she had clearly done her best with bright cushions and vases of flowers, but where the wallpaper was faded and the ceilings blotched by old damp. There was a tiny kitchen and a bedroom with a shower-closet curtained off, at all of which Cesare looked with obvious disapproval.

'The place badly needs decorating,' he told its tenant.

She agreed. 'I have asked again and again, but nothing is done.'

'Who is your landlord?'

She told him and he nodded. 'I know the man, and he is notorious.' He turned to Dinah. 'You can't move in here. It's unthinkable. For one thing, you'd find the heat just under the roof unbearable, not to mention the deplorable state of repair.'

But Dinah, moved by the shadow of dismay which had crossed the other girl's face, said stoutly, 'It's not so bad. It's as compact as a doll's house, and I

49

shall hardly ever be in it in the worst heat of the day. Besides, there's a balcony outside the bedroom window. I could sit out on that.'

Cesare made a further inspection. 'That's no balcony. It's the top platform of the emergency stairs. No doubt you could fry an egg on its iron surface, but there's no room on it to put a chair,' he said, and to Signorina Pacelli, 'No, I'm sorry, but Signorina Fleming must look elsewhere.'

'But——?' The girl looked bewilderedly from Dinah to him, and Dinah said quickly, 'No, it will do. I'm not likely to find anywhere else as convenient for the office, and I shall be very comfortable here. I'll take it, *signorina*, from the date we arranged.'

With a distinct air of relief the other girl said, 'Thank you. I shall leave everything neat and prepared for you, and the key with the porter, whose lodge is next door.'

They exchanged a few more perfunctory words, then Dinah and Cesare left. On the way down he said, 'I suppose I had to expect that piece of self-assertion, hadn't I?'

'I wasn't just being contrary,' she protested. 'I'm the one who'll be living there, and I can. I couldn't go back on my word to take the place; Signorina Pacelli will have to go on paying the rent if she can't find another tenant, and she has very little time left now.'

'It's a slum,' said Cesare flatly.

'You think so? I've seen worse,' she retorted, her tone flippant.

He looked at her sourly. 'Now you *are* being contrary for the sake of it! I'll accept your magnanimity in keeping your promise to take the place, but inwardly you were appalled, don't deny it,' he accused.

Dinah could not in truth, so she said nothing. At the doorway to the courtyard someone else was coming in; it was Trevor Land. Dinah introduced him to Cesare and explained the latter's escorting of her. Trevor asked, 'You have seen the apartment? What do you think of it?'

'Well——' she hesitated, and Cesare countered, 'Have *you* seen it then? Do you approve it?'

Trevor said, 'I looked it over before Dinah came out, and it seemed to me that it should suit her. It's within ten minutes' walk of Plenair, and it's pretty typical of any small apartment in the city.'

'Let's hope not,' Cesare muttered. 'It's a claustrophobic prison cell.'

'Which, as I don't suffer from claustrophobia, doesn't worry me,' said Dinah, feeling it was time she took a hand. 'I've told Signorina Pacelli I'll take it.'

'That's good.' Looking relieved, Trevor added, 'I thought I should find you here, and that if you were, you might lunch with me.'

But Dinah was glad she could plead a hairdressing date. Lunching with Trevor, she now knew by experience, meant his daily haunt of the Ostia Grillo, where the choices on the menu never varied and where the only view was of a sluggish canal.

'We're dining together tonight anyway,' she reminded Trevor.

'At my place, yes,' he agreed. 'I'll call for you.'

They all went together to where the launch was moored, and when Trevor had left them Cesare asked the whereabouts of Dinah's hairdresser's salon. She told him and he offered to drop her there, and when they were aboard he was ready with questions.

'This Trevor Land—he is the colleague you already knew in England?' he asked.

'You remember my mentioning him? Yes,' Dinah said.

'And you see him frequently now?'

'Now and then we lunch together.'

'And you dine with him in his apartment?'

'At the guest-house where he lives,' she corrected. 'There's a communal dining-room.' I've been there once before.'

'You know him well enough to have let him approve for you that place we've just seen?'

'You could say that, yes. He knew more or less what I wanted, I respect his judgment and I was. grateful that he could help me.'

'What a sober testimonial!' Cesare mocked. 'From which, I suppose, one has no right to conclude that for you he is the one Englishman for whom you claim you would reject all Italians?'

She felt her colour rise. 'No right at all,' she said.

Silence followed that until he pulled in to the quay she wanted and he helped her out. Then he prompted, 'Haven't you forgotten something?'

'Forgotten? What?'

'Surely? Just the classic get-out clause to any denial of romantic involvement—namely, "We are just good friends." ' He grinned over his shoulder as he sent the launch scudding away.

Trevor's lodgings were across the lagoon, just off the Zattere waterfront. The short journey was only one stage of the *vaporetto*, and he escorted Dinah back the same way after calling for her that evening.

The dinner menu was homely but appetising, and afterwards they took coffee and sat on in the little walled garden behind the house. Even until quite late the air was stifling and Dinah thought longingly of a trip somewhere by water. But Trevor had problems to discuss and seemed disinclined to move.

He had had a trying day at the office; he had had to make two decisions which he wasn't sure his chief would approve; two of the desk staff had gone sick, and Etta Megio——

'You know Etta, my secretary?' he paused to ask Dinah. 'Yes, well, she's being very difficult lately; her work is falling off, she doesn't take the keen interest she used to, and I've heard her being very short with clients, which obviously one cannot have.'

'Perhaps she's tired, in need of a holiday,' Dinah offered. 'When is she due for one?'

'Oh not yet—not until after the seasonal rush. But if she doesn't show up better than she has done lately, I may have to consider demoting her and taking on someone more reliable.'

'She won't like that,' said Dinah, suspecting she could guess at Etta's trouble.

Trevor agreed, 'Well, of course not. Who would? And as we've got on very well together so far, I'd be quite reluctant to do it.'

'Has she a boy-friend?' Dinah asked.

'You mean she might be having trouble with him? But I don't think she has.'

'Well, have you tried taking her out sometimes yourself? I don't mean just to lunch at the Ostia Grillo, but, say, an evening on the town—somewhere gay; make a bit of whoopee?'

Trevor registered mild shock and disapproval of the suggestion. 'Even if that were the solution, it wouldn't do at all,' he said. 'In my position I can't single out one of the junior female staff for particular attention of that sort. Besides, *you* wouldn't care about it, would you?'

'If I were going to be jealous, I doubt if I'd have suggested it.' In fact, rivalry with Etta for Trevor hadn't entered Dinah's head and now she wondered why not. She *ought* to be disturbed and a little jealous, oughtn't she? If you were in love with a man you couldn't be genuinely so generous with his attentions to other girls, could you? She wished she knew more certainly how she herself stood with Trevor—whether he desired her as a woman as much as he seemed to value her companionship and as a colleague. If he kissed her more often or voiced their future plans which he seemed to take for granted, she would know. But without more ardour on his part, she couldn't measure her own.

Trevor was saying now, 'I suppose you wouldn't talk to her? Find out what's wrong with her work, I mean?'

Jerked back from her thoughts, Dinah echoed, ' "Her"? Oh—Etta? Do you think that would be a very good idea?'

'I don't see why not,' he said. 'She might be prepared to confide in another girl things which she wouldn't tell me, so would you try?'

'All right. But don't be surprised if I have to report back that she claims there's nothing wrong, or that if there is, she doesn't agree it affects her work. Shall I ask her to lunch with me one day, perhaps?'

'Good idea. At the Grillo?'

Dinah suppressed a shudder. 'No. I'll invite her to bring a packed lunch, as I will too, and we'll meet in the Gardens. Leave it to me.'

Later that night, on the short distance between the *vaporetto* landing stage and the Palazzo d'Orio, Trevor put his arm round her shoulders and they walked as intimately entwined as were the few other young couples they met. But then, and also when he kissed her goodnight, Dinah was dismayed by the little response she felt or was able to show.

This was what she had thought she wanted, wasn't it?—for Trevor to play the lover and she the courted? He hadn't kissed her as ardently since she came to Venice, but where was the leaping pulse which she had expected would reply? It wasn't there; it didn't beat for him, and what was even worse, he didn't even seem to notice!

It was a problem she knew she was going to have

to face. If they were to marry ultimately he must not take her for granted, and she must know what it was to thrill to him, to his voice, to his touch. There had to be a magic which sparked. For without it there was nothing.

When she invited Etta, the girl's response was so lack-lustre that Dinah wondered if she would keep the rendezvous. But she did, and they found a shady corner in the Public Gardens away from the mid-day crowds. They exchanged items of the food they had brought with them, but Etta only toyed with hers before she asked, 'Why did you ask me out? You don't know me at all well. You must have had a reason?'

Dinah decided on the truth. 'It was your chief who suggested I should,' she said, and watched the girl scowl.

'And what reason had *he*?' she demanded.

'He is worried about you, about your work which isn't as good as it was, he says. And if there were any cause for that, he thought you might be more willing to talk to me about it than to him.'

Etta's chin went up. 'Talk to *you*, *signorina*? The very last person I should choose for my confidante!' she scorned.

There was a pause before Dinah questioned gently, 'I wonder if I can guess why? Could it be because you believe I am closer to Signor Land than you care to think?'

Etta looked away. 'What does it matter to me how close you are to him?'

Dinah said, 'I think it could, if you are growing

fond of him yourself. I admit we've known each other for a long time and we are good friends, and we were glad to be meeting here again in Venice——'

'*And* there is an understanding between you?' Etta accused.

'If by an understanding you mean an engagement —no.'

'But there will be?'

'I don't know.' With a wry recollection of Cesare's taunt, Dinah added, 'For the moment, all we are is just good˙friends.' (What a very useful phrase it was, after all!)

'He engaged and approved Maria Pacelli's apartment for you, even though, when you went in to see it, you went with another man!'

Surprised, Dinah asked, 'How do you know?'

'Signor Land mentioned it. I think he was hurt.'

Dinah shook her head. 'I don't think so, and the other man was only Signor Vidal, the cousin of the two youngsters I brought out from England with me. He had given me a lift in his launch.'

'Signor Vidal! All Venice knows him for what he is. No wonder Trevor—Signor Land—was offended!'

Dinah decided she didn't want to hear again what 'all Venice' knew to Cesare's detriment. With more rebuke in her tone than she intended, she said, 'There's no wonder about it at all. Trevor couldn't have been offended, and wasn't, I know. And please call him Trevor to me, if you think of him so. But aren't we getting away from the subject—discussing my affairs, instead of his worry about your work?'

'And that's my affair, isn't it?'

'Is it altogether, if he is dissatisfied with it, and we are agreed that your worry over me could be the cause?'

'Who is agreed?' Etta demanded. 'You two have been discussing me—laughing at me for—for being in love with him and being over-anxious to please him . . . and failing!'

'I meant,' Dinah explained patiently, 'that you and I are agreed, as I think we are. He knows nothing of your feelings for him, and I promise you I won't break your confidence.'

'Then why are you questioning me?' asked Etta shrewdly.

'I told you—because he is worried about you. He likes you; until now he has been able to rely on you, and he doesn't want to replace you by someone else.'

'Perhaps,' Etta hesitated with a quiver of her lip —'it might be better if he did; if I hadn't to see him every day, knowing——'

'It might be,' Dinah allowed. 'But that would make you very unhappy, wouldn't it? No, I think you should go on as you are and determine to be worth his reliance on you, and—hope.'

'How can I hope for what I want of him, when it is you he wants?'

Dinah said slowly, 'But I don't know that he does, in the way I think I need to be wanted.'

'But you want him?'

'I don't know that either.'

'And that is why you think I may hope?'

Dinah shook her head. 'It doesn't follow that if he doesn't love me, he'll love you. Things don't work out so neatly,' she warned.

'But if I am there, and make myself valuable to him?'

'It could happen.' In that moment Dinah suspected that she felt less for Trevor than this girl did, and she made a resolve that until she was more sure that to lose him or be lost by him would matter deeply to either of them, she would see less of him; give them both a chance to miss each other. If they were going to, which she was ready to doubt.

When she and Etta parted she realised Trevor would expect a report on the upshot of their talk and that she had promised the girl she wouldn't betray her confidence That posed a problem, and Dinah wasn't to know then that when he did put the question to her he was going to be satisfied with her evasion that Etta had seemed shocked at his criticism of her work and that she had been put on her mettle to prove it unjustified.

Meanwhile the twins' holiday time was racing away, but while it was passing they had made Venice their own. Touristwise they had 'done' it thoroughly; they had tramped the floors of the Doges' Palace, shuddered at the chill of its dungeons, marvelled at the ancient wonders of St Mark's, looked down on the city from the heights of the Clock Tower and the Campanile, bought an expensive trip in a gondola, shopped for souvenirs and home-gifts on the Rialto Bridge, and made the Lido their almost daily playground.

They got themselves invited to beach parties and picnics on the Brenta, and treasure-hunts in the back streets and mazes of *riva* and *calle* and *campo* —the quays and alleys and squares where feet were the only transport and handcarts the only vehicles. Towards the end of their stay they brought to Dinah the problem of their return of hospitality. They simply *must* give a party. But how? If they suggested holding it at the Palazzo d'Orio, did Dinah think Cesare would 'play'?

'If we arranged all the catering ourselves?'

'If we hired a radiogram, so as not to use his, and people brought their own favourite discs.'

'If we promised not to let the scene get too rowdy?'

'If we asked him and his precious Princess— which would be a bind, but we would—what do you think? And would you ask him for us?' they wanted to know.

Without any experience of how Cesare was likely to react to the idea, Dinah demurred on the score of expense, upset to the household, the numbers they were likely to invite, and reminded them that the three of them were only there on Cesare's condition that they make no demands on him. To all of which they countered that they still had some of Aunt Ursula's money left, that they only wanted the use of the big *salotto* and the freedom of the kitchens for one night, that the numbers of the guests needn't exceed twenty or—well, say twenty-four, counting themselves, and how could any such self-organised an affair make any trouble at all for Cesare? So would Dinah please ask him and see what he said?

60

Dinah did, and was surprised by his almost casual compliance, though he ruled there was to be no question of their catering or cooking for themselves.

'Tomasa would never stand for it,' he said. 'Tell them to let her know numbers and the kind of things they want, and she will order the lot from Florian.'

'I doubt if they can afford Florian's stuff,' said Dinah.

'The bill can come to me.'

'But it's their party, and they want to pay for it.'

'Then let them pool the money they mean to afford, and I'll take care of the rest. What about drinks?'

'Their favourite tipple is Coke.'

'Well, their Italian friends will expect some wine Have Tomasa order some rosato. How, by the way, have they managed to collect this bevy about them in the time?'

'I think they converged on the beach by some process of magnetic attraction. Like molecules, or whatever does that kind of thing in science,' Dinah smiled. 'By now they know some Germans and Swiss and some other English boys, as well as the original Italian family they got to know. They're inviting you to the party, by the way.'

'And you?'

Unable to resist the irony, Dinah said, 'Oh, I shall be there in my role of Head Wardress, of course. Will you be accepting the invitation?'

'I? *Santo cielo*, no! I shall arrange to have a cast-iron previous engagement, and I'd advise you to do the same.'

'I can't.'

'Why not?' On his way to the door, Cesare paused. 'Tomasa and Giuseppe can mount guard to see that they don't jump in the Canal for a swim, or throw in someone else, or break up the furniture, and I'm sure your Englishman would love to take you out for an evening on the town. Or are you showing off your determination to carry out my conditions to the letter?'

'No,' she said. I'm looking forward to enjoying it.'

He shrugged. 'Good. I only wondered.'

The arrangements for the party went ahead, the number of accepting guests swelling to thirty before even the twins agreed that a halt should be called. The form of the evening was to be talk—some of it necessarily in sign-language—and dancing and a barbecue on the Palazzo's private side-quay. Seating in the *salotto* was no problem since everyone, Lesley asserted, was used to, and preferred, sitting on the floor. And it wasn't going to be *that* kind of a party—where people went berserk and broke things up. What kind of hooligans did Cesare think they were?

Dress was informal. Besides the barbecue there was a buffet of cold 'eats'. The radiogram would play continuously. There was no sitting-out area— couples who wanted to isolate themselves could take a walk along the quays.

The evening opened to rather a shy start, but as it progressed Dinah thought it must be proving the success that Jason and Lesley hoped. It was a polyglot affair, with four languages being spoken and with signs and mime to fill in the gaps. The dance music was the universal rhythm of 'pop' and its lyrics were shouted in chorus at full decibel rating.

In fact noise, Dinah realised amusedly, was the measure of the enjoyment being had by any group at any given time. They screamed, they yelled with laughter, they vied in shouting each other down, the Italians and the Germans the most strident of all. Dinah doubted whether, even at their age, her set had felt the need to be quite so raucous in proving to each other that they were having a good party. She was having a good one herself, but as the night wore on she did begin to crave a little pause. Not too much—not even a few minutes of blessed silence, but just a degree less din was all she asked.

She didn't get it and, as she stood alone near the door while a conga snaked and curvetted round the room, the noise kept her unaware that Cesare had come in and was standing at her side. A clearing of his throat brought her head round in surprise. 'I thought you meant to stay away?' she mouthed, and he mouthed back, 'And I thought I was safe—that it would all be over by now.'

She looked at the dancers. 'In England congas are often a sign that the end is near,' she encouraged him. 'I know it's late, but we've been having such fun that I haven't had the heart to suggest breaking it up.'

'It has been a success, then?'

'Entirely, I think—except for one lack.'

'Which is?'

She grimaced. 'Ear-plugs for ears which would like to be used again! *They* don't seem to realise the power of their lungs, and having to compete, I'm going to be as hoarse as a crow myself tomorrow.'

'Had you contemplated escape?'

'No, and it will soon be over.'

'But the idea appeals? Say a trip in the launch round the islands?' he asked casually.

She stared at him. 'With you?'

'Well, you'd be exchanging one noise for another, but I promise you the hum of the engine wouldn't match this racket.'

She was tempted; oddly excited. 'Well——' she hesitated, which Cesare took for assent and turned her about, a hand on her arm.

She hung back. 'No, I must tell Jason——'

'Don't stop the carnival.' Cesare pointed to a couple sitting on an ottoman. 'Give them the message, tell them to pass it on.'

There was no need to change out of the workmanlike trouser suit she was wearing, but as the jacket sleeves were short he advised a wrap, as it might be cold on the open water. As he helped her into the launch she found herself tempted to an impish, 'What is this—a reward?'

'A reward for what?'

'For diligent attention to my duties, perhaps. In other words, for being a good nanny?'

He looked down at her as he took his seat at the wheel. 'You do make a meal of a situation, don't you? It hadn't occurred to you that *I* couldn't take that Babel, and mere chivalry couldn't leave *you* to it any longer?' he queried.

Rebuked for ungraciousness, she knew she had asked for it.

CHAPTER FOUR

OUT on the open water all was quiet, except for the hum of the launch's engine. So far out and so late there was little traffic; the lanterns on the stanchions which marked the sailing lanes shone out across pond-still water which, parting and churning to the passage of the boat, slid back afterwards to unruffled peace.

There was a crescent sliver of moon lying on its back, its young light not strong enough to dim the stars; a perfect night, its air fresh but not chill, a night which for atmosphere and scene, Dinah knew, would remain etched on her memory.

She didn't know whether Cesare expected her to make conversation, but at one point she mused idly and whimsically, 'I've sometimes wondered, when all the city traffic stops, if it ever does, whether all the canals heave one sigh of relief that at last they can settle down to sleep.'

Cesare said drily, 'You could ask the same question of any autoroute, I suppose. Or any country lane.'

'Of course.'

'And get the same answer—that there's never any complete peace for manmade highways; there'll always be some busybody jogging along them for his own ends, creating a disturbance.'

'As we are now, just for the sake of it?'

'Speak for yourself,' he retorted crisply. 'I usually have some purpose to what I do.'

They had rounded the point of the mainland, leaving the airport to their port side, and presently the dark mass of the island of Murano lay ahead.

'Our glass factory island. Have you been out to it?' Cesare asked.

'Yes, as part of my homework. In an emergency I might have to play courier to it. Plenair does a morning round trip to it and Torcello and Burano, and Trevor Land has been coaching me in a crash course on their history.'

'H'm. Business before or after pleasure?'

She deliberately misunderstood the oblique taunt. 'You could say, I think, that for him business *is* pleasure. He loves his work.'

'You too?'

'I think I'm going to,' she said.

'When do you start at your office?'

'At the end of next week, after Jason and Lesley have gone.'

Presently she broke a silence to say, 'I know you have a tremendous number of interests yourself, but I don't really know what you do.'

'I manage things.'

'Things?'

'The businesses my father made his money on, and some others I have added since.'

'Such as?'

'M'm—fabrics for export, Burano lace, merchant banking, an emergent film company, I have a director's foot in some hotels——'

66

Dinah affected awe. '*All* those since you took over the companies your father left to you?'

'Not all of them. He had worked up a substantial home trade in silk and leather and glass. Only the export angle has been my addition to them.'

'And hotels?' For some reason she felt a little heady, disposed for argument. 'You surprise me! Now I'd have thought you would despise them as conveyor-belts for tourism.'

As if determined against being ruffled, Cesare said, 'Other people than tourists use hotels—business men, politicians, permanent residents. And none of us despises the tourists' money. It's manna from heaven which pays for other things.'

'So it's only the tourists themselves you dislike?'

'Not even them. I only want the balance kept between my city's traditional role and its new one.'

Dinah sighed. 'You do want things both ways, don't you?'

He nodded. 'As far as one man can, I mean to see that Venice gets them both ways.'

After another short silence he said, 'You argue as a man does. That is, quite logically from whatever point of view you are using.'

'Is that a compliment?'

'It was meant to be.'

'Thank you. So how differently do women argue?'

'Without detachment. They can't keep an issue abstract. Like a skilled tennis player, they play the whole court until they drive one into an emotional corner and make the whole thing personal.'

'And which kind of argument do you prefer?'

'Argument for argument's sake—with a man. With a woman it depends on one's mood and on the woman.'

'But with either, as you mentioned once, you always like to win?'

'And whoever in his senses ever went to war without meaning to win?' he retorted, making it one of those questions which would ignore an answer.

For once he left Dinah in agreement with him. For her too, she realised with a sense of discovery, it depended on the man, and that she was contrasting him with Trevor. For too often, when she expressed herself strongly and needed a bit of fight for her convictions, Trevor would listen, and then with a phrase she had come almost to dread, would say, 'Well, yes —this is it,' and would then proceed to put her reasoning into his own words, deflating the whole thing like a pricked balloon. Whereas she expected and got stimulating opposition from Cesare. Also the unspoken promise that they would both survive to fight again another day. She wondered in what kind of mood he might admit to tolerating or even enjoying finding himself in what he called an emotional corner. In that mood, what type of woman could put him there, and how did he escape the manoeuvre? She supposed, by turning on the charm he must possess, if his reputation for feminine conquest were true. But the experience of Cesare playing the gallant was one she hadn't had. Her impact on him, he made clear, was about as stimulating as a surgical dressing. As was his upon her.

Or was it? She remembered her reaction to his

first criticism of her on the Pass. It had not been so much resentment as blame for herself that to him she had not appeared in a better light. Then he had been a stranger whom she expected never to meet again. But between then and when chance had thrown them together again, her thoughts had carried an impression of him—his looks, his manner, his voice, and though, if they had not met again, she would have forgotten him, when they did her awareness of him had deepened. When he was not there she thought of him more often than she did of Trevor, which was, at the least, disturbing.

Trevor 'out of sight, out of mind'? And Cesare Vidal, always intrusive, always demanding and getting her thoughts' attention—surely that was a crazy state of affairs? Before he left England she had been practically engaged to Trevor! Even now, whether or not he loved her, she thought he took their future for granted. Whereas she did not any longer. Because of this man who had laid cool claim to her leisure for his own self-interested ends, and for whom she had no function but that of escort to the twins? She told herself she hoped not, but her honesty feared it might be so.

Fleetingly she thought, 'If he ever made a pass; if he ever kissed me with any show of passion, I should know what he meant to me,'—and then saw the absurdity of envisaging any such likelihood. She was not even a potential conquest to him; she was merely a female who argued like a man!

The launch wove in and out of the miniature archipelago which stood off from the island of Torcello.

Cesare went close inshore and circled it and then set course for the return journey. Presently, out in open water, he cut the engine, allowing the boat to drift at its pleasure, his hand lightly on the wheel now and then.

'Do you suppose the party will be over by the time we get back?' he asked.

Dinah said, Oh, surely? We must have been out for nearly an hour.'

'Better give them a little more grace. 'You're not cold?'

'No.' She looked up at the new moon, easing back in her seat to do so. 'I'm glad to have seen it for the first time out here,' she said idly. 'In England we say it's unlucky to see it through glass.'

Cesare stared up at the moon himself. 'Unlucky? What a very negative approach!' he murmured.

Dinah laughed. 'Very well—lucky then, to see it out of doors.'

'That's better. Much more positive and cheermaking. Now *we* say, "A growing moon and a lazy tide make a good time for love." So could you approve equally of that?'

What to reply? The only way was to play it lightly. 'I think I'd say of that, that probably only experience could tell,' she answered.

His glance abandoned the moon and came back to her. There was raillery in his tone as he countered, 'Conceding, though, that to gain experience it's necessary to experiment?'

'Yes, perhaps.' Where was this leading? Surely not

70

to the invitation she had decided was unthinkable only a few minutes ago?

But it seemed it was. He dropped his free hand across her shoulders and half-turned to her. She sat rigidly, staring forward, after her first startled glance his way. She knew she had flushed, which he could not see; nor could he guess at the staccato beating of her heart. He mustn't know she had wanted this, half willed it, and now was afraid . . .

He said, 'And so—granted a young moon and a tide as idle as this, should they be denied their rights, would you say?' and without giving her a chance to reply, turned her full towards him, brought his other hand to draw her closer and kissed her with assured purpose in the pressure of his mouth upon hers.

Her own lips remained firm and cool at first, then fluttered in a desire she wanted to deny and could not. A kiss that from him was mere flirtation, but she wanted it to go on and on. She longed to cling, to yield, and she must not. Without the feeling which he did not pretend to have for her, the whole thing was spurious, bogus, and when, slowly, he held her off from him and had kissed each cheek in turn very lightly, she turned her head aside.

Both hands once more on the wheel, he righted the uncontrolled circling of the launch, but did not switch the engine on. Except for the lapping of the water the silence was intense. Then Dinah said in a small choked voice, 'You make the most of your opportunities, don't you?'

'Those which offer only once a lunar month—yes, why not?' he retorted.

'Whether or not you expect any response?'

'But there has to *be* a response!' His tone implied she had asked a foolish question. 'Either one's overtures are accepted or rejected—simple. If they're accepted, there's the chance of going on from there. If they are rejected——'

'Then, I suppose, you can promise yourself that there will be another new moon next month?'

'Exactly. Always supposing there's a pretty girl handy, and that the tide isn't racing.' He laughed suddenly. 'Tch—you are very English, aren't you, Dinah Fleming? Haven't you ever heard of us Italians that we are romantically venturesome to our fingertips; that it's a matter of male honour with us to chance our arm? No offence meant; only a bit of homage at which you should be flattered.'

'Even when——' Dinah's need at the moment was to guard herself from herself as much as from him—'Even when,' she repeated, 'in my case, I thought you understood—you've always assumed so —that I don't happen to be just any handy, footloose girl who might or might not play along with you in your moon-and-tide fairytale; that, on the contrary, I'm more or less committed elsewhere?'

As soon as the words were out, she was appalled. What had she told him for stupid pride's sake? The very thing she had earlier been at pains to deny; the thing which wasn't true—that Trevor was as important to her as Cesare had taunted! So what was he going to believe now—that she was as good as engaged to Trevor, or that she wasn't? She was to know

72

when he drew himself together and bent to turn the engine switch. His tone sober, distant, he said,

'That I didn't understand.'

She couldn't recant now. She had to carry it through. 'After you met Trevor Land you claimed to think it,' she reminded him. 'And would you have behaved any differently, if you had?'

'I might have been tempted, but let's hope I could have told the moon and the tide, "Get thee behind me," as one is supposed to abjure the devil!' He hunched his shoulders and dropped them in the course of a long sigh. Adding his favourite Italian expletive to his perfect colloquial English, he murmured, 'Santo cielo, what a to-do about a mere kiss with obviously no future to it!'

If he weren't to think her the complete prude, she had to go along with that. 'You're right—I'm making a fuss about nothing,' she agreed, dismissing as lightly as he a moment which for her had been sweet . . . too sweet.

His next remark after a silence was entirely matter-of-fact. 'When exactly do Jason and Lesley go back to England?' he asked.

She told him the day and the date.

'And how are they travelling?'

'The same way as we came—by road.'

'Indeed, they are *not* !'

'What do you mean? They have to get the car back home.'

'Well, they aren't undertaking that journey alone. I can't think how you can have considered it.'

Though she had had misgivings herself, Dinah was

surprised by his vehemence. 'But they have to go, and I can't go with them,' she said.

'But you brought them out here, knowing you couldn't see them safely back. It's a problem you should have faced before you set out,' he reproved.

She felt that to be unjust. 'And so I did. But they wouldn't. They said they'd have learned all the snags on the outward journey, and they would be all right.'

'And you listened to them!' he scoffed. 'However, they are now going to hear from me, if not from you, that the scheme is not on.'

'If you say so, of course I'll tell them you forbid it. Though how——'

'They will have to fly or go by train,' he ruled crisply.

'And abandon the car? It would break Jason's heart. Besides, they can't afford to fly. The train would be pretty expensive too.'

'The cost needn't worry them.'

'You mean, you would pay? I'm afraid they would hate that, and they're going to be terribly disappointed at not being allowed to drive back the way we came.'

He glanced down at her briefly. 'And you are going to be at the receiving end of their disappointment?' he queried.

She nodded. 'I probably shall be, until they understand that it's your concern for them that has made you forbid it. They're not monsters. They'll see the reason in that.'

'They'd better.' He paused. Then he conceded,

'Well, if they are so set on the idea, perhaps one can compromise.'

'Compromise? How?'

'Hunt up a convoy for them. Responsible people, going north by car the same way, who would play escort to their car. It could be possible to find some. I'll make inquiries around.'

'I could ask at Plenair. They might know of someone,' Dinah offered eagerly.

'Yes. Or—— Anyway, leave it to me.'

They had reached the Palazzo, where now all was quiet; even the evidence of the barbecue on the side quay had been tidied away. Cesare handed Dinah out of the launch and they went in together. There was a message for him on the telephone pad and while he read it Dinah looked in at the *salotto* and the dining-room, where almost all the ravages of the party had also been cleared away. There was no sign nor sound of the twins, from which she concluded they had gone to bed, and after saying goodnight to Cesare, and thanking him for the trip, she went too.

She was pleased with the twins. If they had been less responsible than they were, the aftermath of the abandon of that party could have been a shambles. But she had her own thoughts of the night to analyse, and she was less than pleased to find both of them in pyjamas sitting cross-legged on her bed, awaiting her.

'Well, there you are!' stated Jason obviously, and Lesley said, 'We got rid of the folks not too long after Yvette and Jules sang that you had gone out with Cesare, and since then we've slaved to put the place in order again.'

'Good for you. I noticed. Was the party a success?' asked Dinah.

'Super!'

'Everyone said so—the best they had been to this summer.'

'We didn't burn so much as a sausage on the barbecue.'

'And none of the neighbours complained. They even turned out to watch. Where did Cesare take you?'

'Out on the lagoon, right round the islands and back. There's a new moon. I hope you saw it while you were outside at the barbecue!'

'For luck, you mean? Pff—who needs mere luck?' Jason scoffed.

Lesley said more soberly, '*We* could on our journey home, without Dinah along.'

'Yes, well——' Dinah had just decided to keep her dampening piece of news until the morning when Lesley broke in, 'Oh, and that princess of Cesare's rang up for him, and was she mad when she heard he had gone out with you? Oh, boy!'

'How do you know? Did you answer the phone, then?' asked Dinah.

'Jason did, but she was gabbling Italian at such a rate that we had to get Gio Conti to listen and translate for us, and he got it all. Seems she understood Cesare had been playing bridge at the Inter-Nation Club, but she had expected he would be home by then, and when we prompted Gio to tell her he'd been back, she wanted to know why he should have gone out again with you. Which of course we couldn't tell her—just that he had, that was all.'

'Oh——' Dinah said blankly. 'I suppose you left a message for Cesare to say she'd called?'

'Yes. By the telephone. He couldn't have missed it.'

Dinah nodded. 'I think I saw him reading it. But your friend Gio must have been mistaken that she minded his having taken me out.'

'Not so. Pretty green-eyed about it, she sounded to me,' Jason remarked.

Lesley regarded him, frowning. 'Do we know what colour her eyes are? And how could anyone *sound* green-eyed?' At which Jason abandoned his cross-legged pose to roll over on his stomach and beat at Dinah's pillow with both fists. 'For pity's sake,' he moaned, 'who, I ask myself, gave me such a moron for a sister, and made her my twin soul at that? Ever heard of green-eyed jealousy, woodentop—no?'

Light appeared to dawn upon Lesley. 'Oh, you mean her Highness was jealous of Dinah with Cesare? M'm, could be——'

'It could *not*,' Dinah cut in crisply. 'The Princess must have been annoyed with Cesare about something else. And now, if you don't mind, I'd soon like the use of my bed, and it wouldn't be such a bad idea if you went back to your own.'

At that they uncoiled themselves, stretched elaborately and went. But Lesley paused to look back round the door. 'What did you and Cesare talk about? Did you fight?' she asked curiously.

'No.'

'What, then?'

'I'll tell you tomorrow,' promised Dinah, depressed for them at the thought, doubting as she did whether either Cesare or the resources of Plenair could produce the necessary escort for them on the day they had to travel. And she knew Cesare would be adamant against their going alone. Odd, she thought, how airily he had sloughed off the lesser responsibilities for them, and yet assumed the deeper care for them which made him deny them the risks of this trip.

Left alone, she faced what she had learned of herself during the evening. She knew now why she thought less about Trevor than she did about Cesare; why she looked forward more to even brief encounters with Cesare than she ever did to arranged meetings with Trevor. it was because Trevor had increasingly turned into a cardboard figure, a familiar shape, with familiar mannerisms and almost wholly predictable reactions. Whereas Cesare was volatile as quicksilver, totally unexpected...exciting. Even in argument with him she felt her mind was at full stretch, and when he had kissed her, every nerve had wakened and thrilled to his magnetism. To even her everyday contacts with him there was a kind of fearful joy, not unlike the tingling anticipation of an exam or any ordeal at which she might fail or succeed. He stimulated her mind, and her body was aware, alight. And that was dangerous. Caring nothing for her, he must not guess how important he had become to her. Pride alone must see to that. She was not going to join the ranks of the 'pretty girls' he had kissed in experiment, some of whom, no doubt, knew and accepted that they stood nowhere with him. But there would have been others who had hoped and dreamed, and she was in peril of that, if she didn't stand back now from the brink of loving him. And given the will, there was still time for that—wasn't there?

As was to be expected, Jason and Lesley were much aggrieved by the news of Cesare's veto on their journey across Europe alone, and were only appeased by his telling them they were free to go ahead with their preparations for leaving as if he hadn't called the ban.

This they did by going round to say goodbye to all the places where they had most enjoyed them- selves, by amassing a collection of absurd toys and mementoes from their friends and by offering to pay themselves for a transatlantic call to their Aunt Ursula to say, 'Thank you for having us—even if you weren't here. And may we come again next year?'

The call was made, Cesare soothing their scruples against his paying for it by saying he would combine it with a talk of his own to his mother, and that the bill would go on his account anyway. They stood over him while he got the connection and talked, then, with frequent passing of the receiver back and forth between them, they put over their own messages and finally beckoned to Dinah—'She wants to speak to you.'

Ursula Vidal's voice was pleasantly English, touched with Italian inflections. She said, 'So you are Dinah who saw my sister Heather's youngsters safely to Venice? I have to thank you so much.'

'It was nothing,' said Dinah. 'I had to come over myself to a job, and we enjoyed a hilarous journey.'

'Yes, so the children said when they wrote—about your coming to work in the city. So that means you won't be going back with them when they go?'

'No, but Cesare hopes to arrange an escort for them in their car, and if he can they'll be quite safe.'

'I'm sure of it. And you are still there with them at the Palazzo, yes? What do you think of our home?'

'It's lovely. Quite different from any other house I've ever lived in.'

'And my bad but attractive and brilliant son—how do you regard him?'

Dinah glanced across at Cesare. 'He is here and listening, *signora*, so what can I say?' she replied.

There was a gay laugh at the other end of the line. 'Which means that you find him all these things and do not want him to know it? Very well. Understood. Though if he is overhearing you, your refusal to reply must already have told him that I had asked what you think of him.'

Feeling trapped by this shrewd reasoning, Dinah hadn't decided on an answer to it when Cesare strode over, made a gesture at the receiver and took it from her.

'Cesare again,' he said. 'And if you were asking friend Dinah for a report on me, I think I can tell you myself that she considers me opinionated, sometimes obstructive and opportunist to a degree.' He listened. Then, 'How well you know me! Yes, I'm afraid I did.' The line crackled again with talk, to which, after listening to it, he said, 'Ah, that, Mother dear, must remain my business. So goodnight to you and sweet dreams. *Ciao*,' and he replaced the receiver.

Dinah could find nothing to say. Jason protested mildly,' 'Did you have to give Aunt Ursula quite such a brush-off? And you could have let Dinah finish.' And Lesley, glancing from Cesare to Dinah, said, 'Whatever all that was in aid of, it's made Dinah blush. And whatever it was, it sounded madly mysterious, I must say.'

'Did it? Good. That happened to be the intention,' said Cesare over his shoulder, already on his way somewhere else.

Left with the twins, Dinah was short with their curiosity. 'Well, with the person in question present, how *do* you say what you think of them off the cuff, just like that?' she countered. And how did *she* know what question Signora Vidal had asked Cesare, to which he had refused her an answer? And of course she hadn't blushed. Or if she had, it had been with embarrassment at being discussed over the phone like that. Most of which may have sounded more annoyed than convincing, but it was the best she could do.

It was not until the day before the twins were due to travel that Cesare produced a plan which he outlined to them, characteristically assuming that it was acceptable to all concerned.

'I shall escort you as far as Lausanne,' he said. 'Dinah will come too——'

'Dinah can? For the ride? Good-*ee*!'

'——where we shall stay the night with business col-

81

leagues of mine. We shall have broken the journey tomorrow night at Domodossola. After the Lausanne night, you will leave early the next morning in the company of Rupert Brissac, my friend's son, who is travelling in his own car to England, and you should make it with one, or at most two, stops on the way. I have business in Lausanne which will keep me until about noon, but on the way back I plan to make the break at Milan instead of Domodossola, reaching Venice again on Sunday evening.'

Dinah hadn't expected to be of the party and said so. Calculating dates, she also reminded Cesare that she had to begin work at Plenair on the Monday morning. To which he promised she would be back on Sunday without fail, adding, 'I like company on a long trip,' making that sufficient reason for his inviting her.

'And we can go over the top of the Simplon, as we did coming out?' Lesley begged.

'On *your* way, if you like. Coming back, Dinah and I will use the Tunnel. It's what it's there for,' Cesare said.

Giuseppe took them all in the launch to the car park and Cesare gave him directions as to the approximate time for meeting him and Dinah on Sunday night. Then the convoy, Cesare matching the speed of his car to that of the Mini, took to the autostrada and the long stretch of the Lombardy plain. Whenever they left the cars and joined company for a rest or a meal, the twins were in regretful and reminiscent mood.

'Wish we were going the other way, instead of heading for home.'

'D'you remember what happened on that bit of road?'

'And where we met the bullock cart, and it was too narrow to get by, and the old man wouldn't budge, and we had to back up for *miles*?'

They were all glad of their beds in Domodossola, and they made the summit of the Simplon the next morning.

'It's not so far down now to that steep bit where we boiled, and you made us all feel like fools for lifting the bonnet,' the twins reminded Cesare. 'Bet if anyone had told you then that we were all going to meet again, you would have said rubbish, or words to that effect?'

'As I felt about you then, I'd more probably have said Heaven forbid,' he replied drily.

'But when we showed up on your doorstep, you didn't turn us out, did you?' Jason questioned.

'Though he was quite brutal with Dinah about refusing to keep us if she wouldn't stay too,' added Lesley.

Cesare looked at Dinah, eyebrows crooked upward. 'Brutal—was I?' he asked.

This time she couldn't deny she was blushing—with chagrin. She looked away. 'I didn't tell them so,' she said.

'What then?'

'I don't remember. Just that—you'd insisted on my staying.'

'But you *thought* "brutal"?' he taunted, seeming

to enjoy her discomfiture. But she was saved from having to reply by Jason's urging of him, 'Anyway, you've taken to us now? You do think we're all reasonably nice people to know?'

They had left the cars for a view of the far blue mountains on the horizon, but now Cesare returned to his and opened Dinah's door for her. 'Let's say you improve on acquaintance, and none of you has the nuisance value I expected,' he said.

Both twins seemed to regard this as an honourable amend.

CHAPTER FIVE

THE next morning Dinah was up early enough to see Jason and Lesley away at first light with their new escort. Previously she had wondered aloud to Cesare that, going to England on his father's business, Rupert Brissac had not chosen to go by air, and she was struck by Cesare's bland reply that the young man had 'obliged' him by escorting the twins. Evidently Cesare's influence ranged far!

The two had gone off reasonably cheerfully, consoled that they had yet more travel to look forward to, and by the prestige they were going to collect from their friends for their having crossed Europe both ways on their own (more or less) in a secondhand Mini far past its first youth.

Dinah had sent presents to her parents by them—fine Italian kid gloves for her mother and bedroom slippers for her father—and she had flowers sent to Madame Brissac from a florist's before keeping her noon appointment with Cesare at the Lausanne Palace Hotel.

She was early for it; he was rather late and suggested they were on their way at once, stopping for luncheon somewhere on the way.

The road ran for some way by the lakeside, past Vevey and Montreux, where they lunched, and Chillon with its grim water-girt castle. Then it began to climb, almost imperceptibly at first, as it took to the foothills and then the heights. The big car did not labour as the Mini had done. It sped along the rare levels and swung smoothly round hairpin bends, Cesare calculating that in four hours they would reach Simplon, and once through the Tunnel by train, they should arrive in Milan by ten o'clock.

Dinah relaxed, content with the length of a journey for which, unlike her outward one with the twins, she had no responsibility. Instead she told herself she must enjoy every minute of what would probably be her last long hours in Cesare's company, listening, talking, today not at odds with him over anything, and hoping she was proving the undemanding companion he claimed he needed on a long trip. In saying so, his tone had implied that anyone would serve his purpose. But he had chosen her, and he needn't have done, and the beginnings of love could extract pleasure from that.

She remembered too late that she had resolved she mustn't admit to loving him—if by love she meant the quiet delight of speaking his name, seeing him come towards her, hearing his voice and of thrilling to the merest impersonal touch of hand or contact of body. But for these few hours with him she indulged herself a little. He *had* somehow made himself the most important person in her life. But on Monday, after her day's work, she would be packing and leaving the Palazzo d'Orio for good. End of an interlude. End of an empty dream.

After Monday the problem of Trevor would claim her again. And here her dilemma was really twin-horned. After deciding to leave Etta a free field with him, later she had claimed to Cesare that she and Trevor were close, and had thought that a way of defending herself from Cesare's flirtatious overtures would be to appear to cultivate Trevor more, not less.

But she couldn't have it both ways! Either to see less of Trevor for Etta's sake, or to see more of him to show Cesare she wasn't footloose and fair game — which? But at the moment of thinking the question she suddenly realised how little any of it was going to matter to Cesare. After Monday she could see as much or as little of Trevor as she pleased, and Cesare wouldn't know, wouldn't realise he was being 'shown' anything at all.

Once or twice, on the road up to the Simplon, he stopped the car to enable her to enjoy a particularly dramatic view. At one such point at a road bend, a single cottage was perched, and from it an old woman in black had taken her chair across the road the better to look down across the great V of the valley, while she knitted busily, her eyes not on her work, but in long, absent-gazed focus on the view.

They did not disturb her by speaking to her, and when they left she was still gazing and knitting, seemingly unaware that anyone had been there.

Dinah shivered slightly. 'What a lonely place to live! How do you suppose she does?'

Cesare said, 'There's probably a little hill-pasture behind the house where it's possible to keep a goat and perhaps grow a few hardy vegetables and some maize for flour. Or she may have a grown son who can fetch supplies on mule-back or by mule cart from Brigue, which would be their nearest township.'

'But imagine the winters up here! What would she do, all the length of them?'

Cesare laughed shortly. 'She lights her lamp, draws up her chair to the fire and goes on knitting, I daresay.'

'No more of a life than that?' Dinah said pityingly.

'You don't know that she hasn't *had* more of a life than that. She may have sailed the seven seas with her sailor husband. Or danced the can-can in a go-go troupe. Or nursed soldiers in some wars. She was as young as you once, remember. And when she looked so absorbed just now, she may have been remembering. There's a poem about old women like her by Ronsard, the French poet. It begins,

"Quand tu seras bien vieille, le soir, à la chandelle..." '

Dinah nodded. 'I know it. The Irish poet, Yeats, made a fairly free translation of it——

"When you are old and grey and full of sleep,

And nodding by the fire——" '

'And does he tell her to remember, as Ronsard did, that she was beautiful when she was young?'

'Yes.'

'And loved?'

'Yes.'

'How?'

Dinah thought. She said hesitantly, 'Something like—"But one man loved the pilgrim soul in you;

and loved the shadows ..." is that it? ... "of your changing face." '

There was a small silence. Then Cesare said, 'Well, there you are. It'll come to all of you in time.'

'Being old, you mean?'

'And being able to remember having been loved by someone.'

Not looking at him, she said, 'Is that going to help, if the loving hadn't been a mutual thing?'

'If the man in question had left you unmoved? In that case, you won't waste daydreams on him years later, I imagine. You're only going to be nostalgic about the one—or ones—who did turn you on, or whatever the jargon for it will be in those days.'

'You make it sound as if we could all count our admirers by computer! For most of us it isn't so, I assure you.'

'Though most of you would have us believe it for discipline's sake,' he retorted. 'Pay any one of you an unwelcome attention, or give her the idea she is being rejected, and she can usually call up a battalion of reserve suitors to her aid.'

'And that's your experience, is it—that we play one man against another in self-defence?'

He nodded. 'In a general way, that's my experience, yes,' he agreed.

'A very wide one, no doubt?' Dinah couldn't resist the barb.

He turned to look at her briefly. 'Wide enough,' he said. 'Wide enough'—and because she guessed he was reminding her of how she had quoted at him her

89

own commitment to Trevor Land, she found herself with no riposte to make.

He had said he liked to win, and he had won again.

Half an hour or so later they reached the terminus of the Tunnel, only to find they had missed a train and there was a long wait for the next. Cesare debated times and distances, and finally decided to drive on over the pass by the same route as they had travelled on the outward journey the previous day.

'Once over the other side, I can reduce our time by taking a short cut to the north of Locarno, and it should make very little difference, if any, to our arrival in Milan,' he claimed.

But there was delay waiting for them. Not far from the point where Cesare had come to the aid of the Mini, an elderly couple were having trouble with their car. They explained to Cesare, when he asked what was wrong, that they had stopped for a picnic meal and when they wanted to go on, the engine had failed to respond.

The driver, hot and harassed, agreed that the cause was probably a flat battery and gratefully accepted Cesare's offer to connect leads and try to charge it from his own engine. But with little result from this move, Cesare decided at last that he must give the other car a tow to the summit where the driver could telephone for garage help and, if necessary, he and his wife could spent the night at the Hospice.

The journey, though not very long, was hazardous and slow, involving much skilled manoeuvring of both cars on the gradients and bends of the road, and Cesare and Dinah had been delayed by nearly two hours before Cesare had completed his Samaritan act and they were on their own way again.

By now it was dusk and there were still several hours' travelling before them. But Cesare claimed he could cut a fair amount from their time by taking the by-road through the lower mountain slopes which he had mentioned to Dinah earlier. 'We shall strike the main road again at Como; from there it will be all autostrada, and we shall have saved two sides of a triangle,' he said.

The road was narrow, and Dinah was glad that she and the twins had not had to negotiate anything like it. Here and there along it were one or two hamlets and one slightly larger township which looked, from its deserted streets and shuttered houses, as if it had already folded itself down for the night. After that the road became no more than a shelf along the mountainside, bordered by towering rock on one side and deep ravines on the other. The night was overcast, fully dark before its time. Appearing like slanting steel rods in the light of the headlamps, rain began to fall, blurring the windscreen and making a morass of the pitted road surface.

The going became rougher; the car rocked and bumped from one pothole to the next; Cesare muttered, 'Sorry about this. I haven't been this way since last summer, when it wasn't soo——'

He broke off sharply as something that was not rain hurtled into the range of the headlights and crashed, splashing, into the puddles. It was a hail of stone; fragments ricocheted onto the car roof to spin

91

away into the ravine; the hail became thicker, more continuous, and then, as Cesare reached for the hand-brake too late, on the bonnet of the car there was a thunder from which Dinah instinctively covered her ears and shrank back, her eyes closed.

She opened them a second later; guessed at the boulder which must have followed the hail, and felt a stab of fear for Cesare, already out of the car, investigating. She slid across into his seat and he spoke to her through the open door, indicating the crumpled metal of the bonnet behind the radiator cap.

'Rock-fall,' he said. 'There should have been warnings out. The radiator may be cracked, but we've got to get away from here fast. And back. There may be worse to come further on, and we can't risk it.'

Taking his seat again, his glance at Dinah and his hand on her shaking knees was solicitous. 'You didn't scream,' he said, stating the fact. 'Did you see the size of the thing which hit us?'

She smiled tremulously. 'I only heard it. I'd shut my eyes,' she said.

'We can count ourselves lucky we weren't a metre or so forward.' Leaving the consequences of that chance to her imagination, he went on, 'Now you had better close your eyes again, for turning on this width of road is going to be tricky.'

But his skill managed it in a single three-point turn. As he drove back by the way they had come, Dinah knew he was watching the instrument panel closely.

She watched it too, and was prepared for his pronouncement, 'The engine is overheating badly. That

92

means no Milan tonight. We can't afford to go any farther than that last place we came through. Frijon. Did you notice if it had a garage?'

Dinah remembered there had been one. 'But it was closed.'

'Then we shall have to knock it up, and also find ourselves a couple of beds for the night.'

A little way short of the village he stopped the car, got out and went to the roadside to lift an object which the headlights had picked out. It was a sign-board, fallen face downward, which read in French and Italian, 'Caution. Danger. Rock-falls ahead. No through road.' Cesare propped it up, secured its base with stones and returned to the car. 'That should keep the next fellow from being too clever, as I was,' he remarked.

On closer view, the garage was obviously a lock-up and they failed to rouse anyone there. Further along the main street an inn-sign swung, creaking, above a shabby doorway—*A l'Aigle d'Or*. 'Let's see what kind of an eyrie the Golden Eagle can offer,' Cesare suggested, and knocked on the door.

Silence. No response. He knocked again and stood back in the roadway to look up at the first-floor windows. Presently a light flickered on up there; a woman put out her head, called *'Un moment,'* and shut the window.

The 'one moment' became several minutes before she came to unbolt the door and to usher them into the hall. Cesare explained their plight and told her they wanted two beds for one night. She nodded,

'*Certainement, monsieur,*' and pointed the way up the stairs.

Dinah, recognising the French and Swiss custom of showing the room to the client before a booking is made, went up with her and Cesare. But she was completely unprepared for the triumph with which the Swiss woman ushered them both into a room containing two beds, saying, '*Voilà, madame, m'sieur!*' with finality.

Cesare's eyebrows went up, and Dinah found her voice. 'Yes, very nice. And—the other room, *madame*?'

A blank look. 'The other one? I have only the one room, *madame*. But two beds—you see?'

Dinah looked at Cesare, who didn't help. 'But——' she began, and the woman regarded her with a puzzled frown. 'You are "family", *madame*? Husband and wife—is it not so?'

Dinah knew she was blushing. 'No,' she said, and belatedly Cesare came to her rescue. He laughed, told the woman, 'You are premature, *madame*. The *signorina* and I are not even engaged!' and told Dinah to accept the room for herself; he would sleep in the car.

She went downstairs with him; he booked her in at the desk, and refused Madame's suggestion that he should sleep on a bench in the bar, saying he wanted to get a mechanic on to the car repair very early, and he would come for Dinah as soon as they could set out again in the morning.

She went to the door with him. For a moment there was a nothingness between them—a kind of vacuum

94

in time. Then he put his lips very lightly to her brow at the hairline.

'That's for *not* screaming, *not* complaining, *not* blaming. It's not an assault on your virtue,' he said of the kiss, and went out.

Dinah was up early the next morning and had to wait some time for coffee and rolls to be brought to her in the inn's austere breakfast-room. She had gone to bed a little bemused by Cesare's unexpected tribute. He criticised so caustically that by contrast his praise was very sweet, and between sleep and frequent waking her mind had mulled over his exact words—her need reading more into them than he could have intended; her fitful dreams making an importance of his kiss. It took the cold sanity of morning to get both words and kiss into focus. He would have commended a child or a younger sister in just that way.

She decided to go to find him at the garage, instead of waiting for him to call for her. She paid her modest bill, hoping he would make no argument about paying it for her, and had bade Madame *au revoir* when the latter asked,

'You did not hear M'sieur return last night?'

'No. Why did he?'

'He wanted to telephone. Me, I was just getting into my bed a second time, and I had to come down again.' Madame gave a resigned shrug. 'However, in this business—that is life.'

Dinah wondered about the telephone call. Since Cesare wouldn't have known overnight how soon the

95

car could be repaired, it wasn't likely he would have been ringing Giuseppe to arrange a new time for the man to meet them with the launch, and it wasn't until they were on their way again, with the repair completed, that Cesare enlightened her.

He asked the same question as Madame had done, explaining, 'I'd hoped to find a kiosk in the town, but I had to come back to the hotel in order to ring Francia Lagna to tell her that I couldn't keep our appointment in Milan last night.'

A cloud obscured Dinah's personal sun. 'You were meeting Princess Lagna in Milan?' she said, not liking the sound the words made.

'Yes. For dinner at The Continentale where I had booked for you and myself, and where she has been staying too, auditioning for a film.'

This was a new and daunting aspect of the Princess. 'Is she a film-star, then?' Dinah asked.

'Not yet. But given the right promotion and the right vehicle for her particular talents, she will be, one hopes.'

Dinah longed to ask what he considered the Princess's 'particular' talents to be. Instead she said, 'And is she expecting to see you in Milan still, even though you couldn't keep your appointment last night?'

Cesare shook his head. 'No. Like most women, she wasn't too pleased over our broken date, and she'll have gone back to Venice this morning by train.'

'But if you hadn't been delayed, I suppose you would have been driving her?' Dinah couldn't resist turning the knife in her own wound.

'That was the idea,' he agreed. 'But as it is, we are going to have to bypass Milan, except for a quick meal, if we are to make Venice at a reasonable hour ourselves.' Which left Dinah to contemplate and be thankful for at least the small mercies both of being spared effacing herself from his tête-à-tête dinner with the Princess last night, and of not having to play an unwanted third on the journey from Milan onwards today. For all her resolution, the plain fact was— she admitted it—she was jealous of Francia Lagna, and on the one or two occasions they had met since their first encounter outside the Royal Danieli, the Princess's manner had been supercilious to a degree. It was small of her to mind, Dinah knew, but her resentment had had allies in the twins.

'Seems to regard Cesare as her exclusive property; that we don't belong to him at all and haven't any right to be here!' Lesley had grumbled darkly on one occasion when the other woman had remarked with pseudo-sweet tolerance that, considering all Cesare's responsibilities, he showed extraordinary patience in shouldering the entertainment of young people, virtually strangers to him, who, she understood, had invited themselves. But that was Cesare all over— generous of his time to a fault.

To which Lesley, using Dinah as reluctant interpreter, had retorted rudely, 'You think so? Well, perhaps you should ask Dinah about that!'—advice which the Princess had loftily ignored.

From Padua Cesare telephoned to tell Giuseppe when to meet them; arrived at the Palazzo, he left again almost immediately, presumably to placate the

Princess over his defection last night, and Dinah ate dinner alone. It would be her last dinner there, she reflected forlornly, missing the twins' spirited company. She meant to pack tonight and to move herself and her belongings, with Trevor's help, into her rented flat after work tomorrow. She hadn't wanted to enlist Trevor, but he had insisted, and just as she was ready for bed, he rang to confirm that she was back and that she would be in good time at the office in the morning.

Sooner or later conversations with Trevor usually became shop talk, and this one was no exception. The manager was back from his holiday; he had praised Trevor's deputising; he would be putting Dinah into the inquiry counter at first; later she would be second-in-charge of Day Tours, and Etta, Dinah would be glad to hear, seemed to have taken to heart whatever Dinah had said to her. Now she couldn't do enough to show interest in her work and his; they were a team again as they had been earlier; he thought even Dinah would notice a change in her.

'And,' he concluded earnestly, 'I really hope she *has* got a boy-friend who is good to her. For I found myself looking at her the other day, and actually, you know, she's quite pretty!'

As Dinah knew from experience, Mondays were apt to be the busiest days of the week in a tourist office, and the Mondays of Plenair were no exception, when its clients, newly arrived from all points on Saturday evening, had had time and leisure on Sunday to debate plans and on Monday descended on their agents in eager droves.

Dinah spent her morning on the inquiry counter, answering questions, directing people to other departments, advising on shopping, explaining the intricacies of the Italian currency, and demonstrating on street-maps the best ways of getting from here to there. There was an English novelist in search of local colour, wanting to know where he could best meet and talk to some gondoliers on their own ground. A French lady, outraged by the prices of Venetian leather goods, had to be soothed and assured that they would be even higher in Paris. A freelance tour guide called to complain that Plenair was poaching his preserves by advertising tours cheaper by a thousand lire than his own. A bachelor on a lone-wolf holiday didn't want anything in particular of Dinah except to ask outright for an evening date. To him she replied with her sweetest smile that she was engaged.

'*Fidanzata o occupata?*' he wanted to know, trying out his Italian.

'Both,' she lied, in order to get rid of him. But when she had no choice but to lunch with Trevor at the Grillo, she decided against reporting this evasive play on words. Busy she was for the evening; betrothed she was not, and for her own reasons she didn't want Trevor to think she had made the claim seriously. The subject of being engaged was one she did not want to bring up with him just now.

It was nearly eight o'clock before they were both free to go to the Palazzo to collect her luggage and take it to the flat. Trevor had hired a water-taxi, and when her things were loaded and while he waited in it, Dinah sought out Cesare.

He brushed off her thanks for his hospitality. 'I made conditions; you accepted them. It's all worked out smoothly; no obligations on either side,' he said.

'I don't agree. Unwelcome guests we may have been at first, but since then you've spared nothing to make us all feel at home.'

'What did you expect? You're not the only one to honour bargains,' he retorted. 'And now, I suppose, you revert to your role of bachelor career woman?'

Irrationally she was hurt by his cool brusquerie. 'You could say that,' she agreed, her voice falling away.

He took the hand she held out to him. 'So what am I to wish you in it?' he asked.

(If only he wouldn't sound so *final*, as if they were never likely to cross paths again! She was still to be in Venice. He was. So surely——?) Aloud she said, 'Well, to hope that I'm going to enjoy it would be— friendly, don't you think?'

'Would it? Then I'm friendly. Take my good wishes as read, won't you? And perhaps we could meet some time, say for an academic argument over luncheon, perhaps? I'll ring you.' He released her hand.

That was all—as politely mannered a parting as she had ever experienced. He wouldn't ring, of course. She had no reason to hope he would.

At that hour the Calle Maser was noisy and crowded with all those of its residents who had escaped the heat in their apartments to gather on the street for an evening gossip. Trevor and Dinah, carrying her luggage from the nearest mooring-basin, were eyed with curiosity, and chatter followed them into the courtyard off the Calle.

Maria Pacelli, who was not leaving for England until the morning, was waiting for them at the door of her apartment. She stood aside after greeting Dinah, who gave a gasp of surprise as she stepped from the vestibule into the living-room.

It had been completely done over. The faded wallpaper had gone, replaced by a deep cream colour-wash; the blotched ceiling was cleanly white. Through a door which stood ajar it was possible to see that the kitchenette had had a similiar treatment. There the walls were a cerulean blue, the woodwork of the fittings a glossy white.

Dinah turned back to meet her young landlady's smile. 'My word, you have done wonders with a pot of paint!' she praised. 'Or did your landlord agree to do it for you?'

Maria Pacelli shook her head. 'I didn't have to ask him,' she said. 'It was your'—she hesitated—'it was Signor Vidal, who was with you when you came to view. He came back the next day, said he had been in touch with my own landlord, who had agreed to the redecoration as long as Signor Vidal paid for it, and the Signore wanted my agreement to put the job in hand.'

Dinah stared. 'But I've seen you since at Plenair, and you didn't say anything about it!'

'He asked me not to. As a friend of yours, he wanted to surprise you.'

'But there was no reason why——' Dinah began as Trevor broke in, 'Why on earth should he have done such a thing for you? You've always said you've found him rather distant!'

There was a note of suspicion in Trevor's tone which irritated Dinah. 'You don't suppose I know why he did it, do you?' she demanded. 'Whatever he may have told Signorina Pacelli, he couldn't have meant it as a pleasant surprise for me. He could only have urged her to secrecy because he must have known I wouldn't have allowed him to do it.'

'Then I did wrong to agree? It embarrasses you, and I should have told you?' Maria Pacelli inquired anxiously.

'Not if you had promised Signor Vidal you wouldn't,' Dinah assured her. 'Besides, the only explanation must be that he was as shocked for you as for me by your landlord's laxity, and so took things into his own hands to benefit us both.'

'He couldn't have had any thought for me in his mind,' the other girl denied quickly. And Trevor muttered, 'Pretty presumptuous of the fellow, if you ask me. What business was it of his?'

Dinah looked about her at the *fait accompli* of the brightened room. 'Well, anyway, it's done, isn't it? So I suppose one must just accept that it has made the place pleasanter for Signorina Pacelli, as well as for me.'

At that Maria Pacelli looked relieved, and after giving Dinah some final instructions and advice, she

102

left to spend her last night with friends. But Trevor was not so easily placated. As he helped Dinah to unpack and arrange her belongings, he suggested, 'You've turned rather complacent, haven't you? Aren't you going to make any protest at all about the man's overstepping himself like this?'

'Of course I mean to ask him why he did it,' she retorted.

'Then you do see how it puts your relationship with him in a questionable light?' Trevor persisted.

'*If* we had the dubious kind of relationship you mean, yes. But we haven't.'

Trevor murmured a perfunctory, 'Sorry,' adding, 'But you are going to ask him what his motives were, I hope?'

Dinah said wearily, 'I've told you I mean to. It has done a lot to make the place presentable, you must admit. But he had no right to go about it so furtively, and particularly not to pretend to Maria Pacelli that he did it as a surprise package just for me.'

There was a pause. Then Trevor questioned diffidently, 'I suppose you wouldn't like me to tackle him for you?'

'No! Why should you?' she snapped so sharply that he made a shrug and a compression of his lips his reply, and they hadn't returned to the subject when he left some time later with his usual parting kiss and a 'See you at the office in the morning, then?' which tonight struck her as a rather bleak reminder of the only 'relationship' they had.

After he had gone she wondered what she had expected or hoped of his reactions to Cesare's quixotic gesture. Would she have been more gratified, or less, if he had followed up his first suspicious protest by insisting she should allow him to get Cesare's explanation at first hand, instead of abandoning his half-hearted offer in face of her sharp refusal to accept it? Somehow she felt let down by his lack of emotional concern for her at the same·time as she felt freed by it. She was weakly feminine enough to want his protection, but from now on she needn't feel guilt that she had as little loyalty to offer him as he had to give her. They had nothing in common but the daily round which had thrown them together, and she suspected he might be as relieved as she was when, some time in the future, they had to acknowledge it as fact.

Meanwhile, if only for the reason that Cesare would look for some move from her, she had to make it. Would she thank him? Yes, she supposed so. But if he expected mere twittering gratitude, he was going to be mistaken! Thanks she would have offered freely, if he hadn't been so devious and cryptic in his methods. What made him think he had the right to 'surprise' her with so high-handed a manoeuvre? Why had he let Maria Pacelli draw her own false conclusions about it? Trevor, too, hadn't been wanting in suspicious reaction, and as Cesare knew Trevor had called at the Palazzo to take her to the flat, he must have guessed Trevor would be there when she first saw how it had been made over. It wasn't fair of Cesare to put her in such an equivocal position. It really wasn't!

She looked at Maria's telephone several times

without summoning the will to use it. And when at last she made to lift the receiver, the bell rang, forestalling her.

'*Pronto*,' she said automatically to a silence on the line before Cesare's voice said in English, 'Well?' on a note of question for which she wasn't prepared.

'Oh——' she said. 'You? I was just going to ring you. That is—I mean, why are you calling me?' The words came out as a babble which she deplored.

Cesare said coolly, 'To hear your approval of my efforts on your behalf, of course. What else?'

'You mean the renovations here? Yess, well—they've done wonders for the place.' She pulled herself together. 'But why had *you* to lay them on, and to tell Signorina Pacelli that they were a personal favour from you to me?'

'Which they were.'

'But where was the need? And for all the secrecy? You must have known how it would look to—to other people; that it would embarrass me to explain it away.'

' "Other people" comprising La Pacelli and——?'

'Trevor Land. You knew he was coming to see me settled in.'

'Yes, of course. News to me, though, that anyone could suppose I planned to furnish a love-nest for you, merely because I wouldn't have you leaving my home for the kind of hovel that apartment was when I viewed it with you. Though little enough could be done for it, I did what I could. It was as simple as that.'

Dinah bristled. 'Then why couldn't you have made

105

it a simple affair of doing it for Maria Pacelli's benefit as much as for mine? As it was, she thought——— They both thought———'

She heard Cesare sigh, whether in simulated or real despair she couldn't tell. He murmured, '*Santo cielo*, you do have some naughty-minded friends! So do allow me to assure them through you that if I really wanted to undermine your virtue, I should do it more subtly than with a pot of paint and a lick of colour-wash. Meanwhile, you haven't thanked me for making the place a bit more habitable. Or don't you care for the colour scheme?'

Despairing of making him take her scruples seriously, she said, 'Of course I'm grateful, and I do thank you. Though I still don't see why you thought it necessary to do it at all. For me, that is, as you say you did.'

'Why not for you?' I haven't any obligations to Signorina Pacelli.'

'Well, have you any to me either?'

'None that I know of. Unless you count your efficient stewardship with my cousins.'

'Well then———?'

'*Well then*,' he mimicked, 'you should give yourself the exercise of thinking of a minimum of six motives I may have had, and by the law of averages you might arrive at the right one.'

This was turning into a fencing-match with words. Dinah said, 'Surely it would save me some trouble if you told me what was the right one?'

'Willingly—if I had any idea of it myself,' he countered, and rang off.

CHAPTER SIX

The routine of Dinah's working day took over. Sometimes she was not able to avoid joining Trevor at the Grillo in the midday break, but as often as she decently could, she took a packed lunch and a book, and went to the Public Gardens. Though the office did not close until half-past seven in the evening, the flat was still hot when she returned to it, and it was then that she most minded her solitary life.

At home there had always been family, friends, something to do by way of recreation, and her stay at the Palazzo had always been enlivened by the twins' active demands on her company. She would not let herself admit to a longing for Cesare's challenging presence, but the contrast of everything about life in his home made the confines of the flat into a prison cell.

Trevor had embarked on a business course in Management which kept him at study in the evenings—a fact which postponed for Dinah a confrontation which she was dreading. Sooner or later she would have to broach the subject of their plans being so indeterminate that they had no right to monopolise each other's leisure time. But while it was Trevor who had to make the excuses for not taking her out, she could agree wholeheartedly with him that work and his chances of promotion must come first, and could salve her conscience at the same time.

Meanwhile Etta seemed fully content with Trevor's preoccupation with work. To be there for him whenever he needed her services appeared to be all she asked, and Dinah wondered when, if ever, he would realise that here was a girl eager to take all that he had never offered to herself; eager to give all that Dinah had not been able to give to him.

The tall houses of the Calle Maser and Dinah's courtyard teemed with life. No one house was occupied by any one family. Each floor housed several, with the inevitable consequence that on hot nights adults and children alike spilled noisily out of doors to continue their talk, their handiwork, their play, until the air cooled sufficiently to send them to their beds.

Dinah's immediate neighbours on her floor were a young grass widow, whose husband was at sea, and an old lady who should never have been marooned on a top floor, since she suffered from a condition which Dinah never heard her describe as other than 'my legs', and she could not easily manage the stairs. Sometimes, when young Signora Forza, driven out by the heat, took her two toddlers downstairs in the evening, Dinah would sit with Signora Benito to keep her company, and both Signora Forza and Dinah did her shopping for her.

Cesare did not ring to make a date. Dinah had not expected he would, though she couldn't quite stifle the hope that he might. Once she saw his name listed among the guests at a civic dinner, and the same journal carried a picture of him with Princess Lagna at his shoulder, the caption reading, 'Signor Cesare Vidal, with friends.'

News of the twins came via the occasional brief scrawl.

Jason (or Lesley) was well; Jason was in college in Reading, Lesley was training at Oxford, so that, with the help of the Mini, they sometimes got together for a day off. How was Venice? Dinah was to give it Jason's (or Lesley's) love. He/she would be back some time. Why had Dinah left the Palazzo in such a rush after they had gone? Surely Cesare hadn't turned her out when he had no further use for her? And was that princess of his still swanning around? Or had he taken up with someone else? If so, serve her right for being so bossy.

The first days of Dinah's isolation became a week, two, three, a month. The tide of tourism ebbed a little, but the great heat held through September into October, and the nightly exodus on to the pavements of the Calle Maser went on. But one evening a sharp torrential downpour sent everyone indoors early, and the staircases and open doorways to the flats took over as meeting-places. The building quietened sooner than usual, as bored children were sent early to bed; the rain had cooled the air a little, and it was easier than usual to sleep at a reasonable hour.

Dinah did not know what time it was, nor what had waked her with a start. She reached for the light-switch without response from it; evidently the storm had fused the connections. Oh well—she was preparing to settle down again when an unfamiliar sound caught her attention and she sat upright, straining to listen.

It was an intermittent crackling sound which became busier—the encouraging sign that a reluctant fire in a grate was beginning to take hold—— *Fire?* Here? In the middle of the night, in grates which either did not exist or had been stuffed with paper decorations for the summer? Dinah felt her blood chill and her legs weaken. For a moment or two she could not move; then she was out of bed and going, barefoot, to open the flat's outer door on to darkness, the continuing crackle and an acrid smell.

The smoke came next, curling experimentally up the stairs, then billowing in clouds as it was fanned by some draught from below. It cleared and fanned out again; cleared, and that time there was a small lick of flame at the lowest stair which Dinah could see before the flight took a turn down to the next floor. And then there was the noise—of doors opening, of excited panic, shouting, of children's cries, and the sinister roar of the fire.

Dinah prayed that someone would have the presence of mind to shut some doors. There was one on the second floor landing which, shut, could prevent the staircase-well acting as a veritable chimney, drawing the fire upward. The noise swelled; people were out in the courtyard now, shouting; Signora Forza was at Dinah's side, peering down the well, clutching Dinah's arm.

'*Miei bambini*,' she breathed. 'They wake and cry in the dark. We must get them out. But how—down there?'

Dinah shook her head. 'I don't know. There is Signora Benito too. How well can she walk if she had to, do you know?'

'She can walk if she must,' Signora Forza confirmed. 'Only step by step, but she can. But my little ones—how?'

'We must try the fire-escape outside my room,' Dinah decided. 'I have a torch. If you'll get the babies, I'll light you down as far as I can, and there must be other people using the escape from the other floors. They will help you, and if you could leave Rosetta and Pietro with someone on the ground, perhaps you could come back or send someone back to help me with Signora Benito?'

'They will be so frightened!'

'Aren't we all?' Dinah murmured in an idiom Signora Forza did not understand. She pushed the girl towards her own room. 'Get them, and *hurry*!' she urged.

Signora Benito was out of bed and tottering bravely. Dinah begged her to wait until the other three had got down; then she went back to light their descent.

Signora Forza went first, carrying baby Rosetta, guiding Pietro's step on to each iron rung. From the second floor platform there came a clamour of voices, and Dinah concluded that from there on the three would have some help.

She coaxed the old lady out of her window and waited, calculating how long it might take Signora Forza to explain what was wanted. While she waited Dinah heard the utterly welcome wail of a fire-float's

111

siren in the distance. 'Listen! The alarm has been given,' she told Signora Benito, who nodded dumbly and achieved a smile.

Signora Forza was coming back. Couldn't she have found a man to volunteer to come in her place? But —this *was* a man. First his head appeared, then his foreshortened body; then he had reached the topmost rungs and was stepping up on to the tiny platform where the three of them made a crowd. What was more, he wasn't just any man, a stranger. He was Cesare.

Dinah drew a long breath of disbelief. How could he be here, at this hour? He looked her over. Though she had hustled Signora Benito into a thick cape and bootees, she had forgotten that she herself was still in her nightgown and barefoot. 'Get something on, and I'll come back for you,' he said. With which he heaved the old lady into a fireman's lift over his shoulder, and steadied himself on the top rung of the iron steps.

Dinah called after him, 'I can make it!' but he gave no sign that he had heard, and by the time she was dressed in pants and a shirt and stout shoes, he was back.

He went down first and she followed safely enough until, a dozen rungs from the ground, she missed her foothold and slid painfully downward, to be caught and steadied by Cesare's hands, firm about her waist.

On the ground the confusion was infinite, the firemen's work hampered by the crowds of onlookers with no more than a goulish interest in the disaster. Dinah's own neighbours were nowhere to be seen.

'I gave the old lady into the care of a hospital squad with a stretcher. And I saw the girl and her two children claimed by some people who took her away,' said Cesare, and then, 'Come along. We can do no good here, as I understand you were the last people to get out. Better leave it to the professionals now. I'll take you home.'

'Home', she guessed, had to be the Palazzo, and when they had pushed clear of the crowds, he explained how he had happened on the scene.

'I'd been at a business dinner on the Calle Verona, and I had moored in the basin near San Fantin——'

'Where you moored, the day you brought me to see the apartment?' Dinah questioned.

'That one, yes. When I came back to the launch there was talk of fire in the Calle Maser, and I went along with the crowd.'

'I was never so glad to see anyone,' she breathed thankfully.

'Though no doubt anyone would have done.'

At the Palazzo she sat resignedly in the hall while Cesare roused Tomasa, who came down, clucking shocked sympathy and offering food and wine, none of which Dinah could face, though she obediently accepted from Cesare a neat Cognac which he insisted she drank.

'She has brought nothing of her own away with her, so make her up a bed and provide her with night clothes and anything else she needs,' he told Tomasa, and to Dinah he said, 'We'll discuss ways and means in the morning. Get to bed now, and sleep if you can.'

'What time is it?' she asked, not knowing.

He looked at his watch. 'Past two. Morning already.'

'The office——?' she hazarded.

'You won't be going,' he decided for her. 'Give me their number and I'll ring them.'

For Dinah there was no routine at all about the next few days.

That first night she had spent, sleepless, in a flannel nightgown contributed by Tomasa, and used a comb abandoned by Lesley for her hair the next morning. Cesare took her to see the devastation of the fire-blackened building, where shutters hung askew; window-frames, empty of glass, stared blindly, and dank, pitiful debris littered the soaked courtyard. The fire had been checked at the second floor, and Dinah was able to go to a nearby school in search of her own belongings among all those which had been rescued and dumped there for the claiming.

There she met Signora Forza on the same errand. Signora Forza had news that Signora Benito was being kept in hospital until a more suitable home than a top floor was found for her. Signora Forza was taking the children to her parents' home in Ravenna.

'And you? Where will you go?' she asked Dinah.

'I shall have to find somewhere else to live. I must advertise, or perhaps someone at Plenair will help,' Dinah said.

She had rung Trevor to tell him where she was, and in the midday break he came to see her, bringing Etta with him.

'Etta thought you might need some things she could

lend you,' he explained. 'What plans have you for moving into another place? Or haven't you had time to think about it yet?'

Dinah thanked Etta, but said that though everything she had brought away with her smelled of smoke, none of her possessions had come to any real harm. She told Trevor the manager of Plenair had given her a week's leave in which to adjust herself, and she would use the time for finding somewhere else.

'You won't stay here,' he said flatly.

'No,' she agreed, equally flatly.

'Well, Etta has a suggestion. Her widowed aunt has a spare room which she would let you have. Would you care to consider that?'

Dinah said she would. 'Where is it?' she asked Etta.

'On the Rio Paglia—just as convenient for the office as the Calle Maser.'

'Thanks. Would you make an appointment with your aunt for me to go to see the room?' asked Dinah, hoping her problem was to be solved so quickly.

But she had reckoned without Cesare's reaction. When she told him of Etta's offer his rejection of the idea was typically direct.

'One room on the Rio Paglia! Have you *seen* the Rio Paglia?' he demanded.

'No. I don't know just where it is.'

'It's a narrow quay on a cul-de-sac canal, and the houses on it just as much fire-traps as that other place.'

'Though is lightning ever supposed to strike twice?'

'Don't be so flippant,' he snapped. 'People, including you, could have lost their lives in that tenement last night.'

Stung by the accusation of 'flippant', Dinah hit back. 'Considering how you claim to care for Venice, you aren't backward in condemning parts of it as slums, are you?' she questioned. 'The Calle Maser; now the Rio Paglia——'

'It's because I know it has slums that I do care,' he retorted. 'If its streets were paved with gold and its buildings were as asceptic as hospital wards, it wouldn't be my city; it wouldn't be Venice. But that aside as an argument for another day, you aren't moving to the Rio Paglia. You are staying here.'

'Here?' Dinah echoed blankly. 'How can I?'

'Why not?'

'Because——' Surely he must know why not!

'Worried that I can't afford to keep you?' he inquired blandly. 'I seem to have managed it before.'

'That was different!'

'Worried then about the proprieties? Why so? Tomasa is a fixture. So is Giuseppe. Between them they can be trusted to chaperon us adequately, don't you think?'

Dinah shook her head. 'I couldn't consider it.'

'Because your Englishman who is only your good friend wouldn't approve the situation for you?'

The very suggestion that Trevor had rights over her decisions acted as a goad. 'My "Englishman",

116

Trevor Land, has nothing whatsoever to do with it,' she said. 'It's I who can't accept. Last night, tonight —while I have nowhere else to go—are one thing. Any other arrangement is out of the question.'

'Though I haven't noticed you have offered any reason of your own as to why it should be,' he pointed out. 'Don't you think you owe me one which I might be prepared to accept?'

She wondered what he would say if she told him, It's because I want to say Yes *too much*. Because I want to be near you again in an everyday way. Because you are tempting me too far, and I mustn't give an inch. Aloud she said lamely, 'You must see I can't be under a continuing obligation to you. Your —friends wouldn't understand it, and it would put me in a very false position.'

'Tchch!' he exploded. 'I thought we agreed there were no obligations on either side!'

'This would make a new one.'

'And what do you think my mother is going to say if you don't accept our hospitality when I am offering it to you, and until she comes home to confirm it herself?'

That brought Dinah up short. 'Are you expecting Signora Vidal back soon, then?' she asked.

'I don't know just when. But very shortly now.' As if he sensed her hesitation he pursued his advantage. 'You see! You aren't prepared to risk her disapproval of me for sending you adrift, are you?'

'I don't know why you should be so insistent that I stay,' she said weakly.

'I miss our academic arguments. I appreciate an opponent worthy of my steel,' he said.

When they heard of it from Dinah, the twins were highly approving of her return to the Palazzo. They each wrote that they had never understood why she had had to leave it when they had come home. Unless (Jason's surmise) Cesare had made a pass at her, and her young man at Plenair had taken umbrage? Or unless (Lesley's) Dinah was no match for the Princess Lagna without them to stand up for her? Which, though the woman *was* sheer poison, had been rather craven of Dinah, and Lesley was glad that the fire-happening and Cesare between them had forced her to go back.

In fact, Dinah contrived to meet the Princess very litte. On most days she did not return to the Palazzo from the office until the evening, and whenever she heard from Tomassa that the Princess would be dining there, she went out to a restaurant herself and did not return until she calculated Cesare and his guest or guests would have gone on to a night club, as often happened. Cesare she saw no more often than when the twins had been there. He too was out all day and only cccasionally dined at home without guests. He and she, Dinah thought, might have been people occupying the same hotel, acknowledging each other over infrequently shared meals, but otherwise their paths not crossing.

So much, she sometimes reflected, for her hopes of his company! So much, also, for her fears of an intimacy which might have been embarrassing. Noth-

ing, in fact could be more correct than their relationship; impossible for anyone to judge differently.

Or so she was able to believe until one Sunday
when, Cesare having gone to friends at Padua, she
had lunched alone at home and the Princess telephoned, asking for her.

'You are not engaged for this afternoon?' Princess
Lagna asked.

'No.'

'Then perhaps you will take afternoon tea with me
at the Gritti Palace?'

The invitation was so unexpected that Dinah
echoed it stupidly. 'The Gritti Palace? This afternoon?'

'Yes. You know it, of course? Then I shall expect
you. At four o'clock. For a little talk——' She rang
off.

Replacing her own receiver, Dinah regretted her
unguarded 'No' which had made it impossible to refuse the invitation later. A 'little talk' had a patron-
ising ring, and she went to the rendezvous feeling like
a schoolgirl arraigned for misbehaviour.

The Princess poured lemon tea, ate nothing herself
and made small pretence of having summoned
Dinah to a mere social occasion.

In her husky, attractive voice she said, 'You are so
elusive that I have had to await my chance to speak
to you without embarrassing you with Cesare. I have
also tried to think, as he said of you at our first meeting, that, being English, you see no evil where in fact
it exists. Or if not evil, at least scandal in the eyes of
others. You understand me, I hope?'

119

Dinah toyed with a minute cream pastry. 'About scandal in relation to myself? No,' she said bluntly.

'No?' Francia Lagna shrugged golden-bronze shoulders. 'What a pity! I thought that by now you must surely be aware of how Cesare's friends—and mine—regard your exploiting of his hospitality for so long and with no excuse, now that his young cousins have gone back to England?'.

Dinah laid down her fork. To eat any more of the absurd pastry would have choked her. 'Meaning, Princess, that Signor Vidal's friends and yours—and you too?—see scandal in my staying at the Palazzo d'Orio at his invitation?'

Another shrug. 'I had hoped that I need not spell it out.'

'But I think you should. What scandal am I inviting, would you say?' Dinah demanded. She knew, only too well. Initially she had feared it herself and had tried to warn Cesare too. But in the event they were both so innocent, so—separate, that the insinuation roused her to fury. She was fighting Cesare's battle as well as her own!

The Princess said, 'You are not a child. You should know that in our country, if not in yours, an unmarried girl does not live in the same house as an unmarried man, unless chaperoned by one of his or her own relatives.'

'But if this is so, shouldn't Signor Vidal know it?' Dinah countered.

'Of course he knows it.'

'Then why should he have risked the opinion of his friends by inviting me to stay until Signora Vidal comes home?'

'*If* he invited you——'

As equably as she could, Dinah said, 'I could hardly have invited myself, could I?'

'By pleading that you had nowhere else to go, you could have made it difficult for him not to invite you after the disaster of your fire.'

'But I *had* somewhere else to go!'

'And if I may say so, *signorina*, disaster does seem to be on your side in helping you to embarrass Cesare, does it not?'

'And what do you mean by that?'

'Well, besides the fire which made you homeless, there was also that timely accident which enabled you to spend a night alone with Cesare in some remote village on the Alpine slopes. You remember?'

Dinah could laugh off the absurdity of that. 'You are not suggesting, surely, that I was able to engineer that piece of misfortune?'

'No, only that you were probably eager to grasp at the chance of several extra night hours in his company, knowing that he had to break a rendezvous with me.'

'That I didn't know until the next morning,' said Dinah. 'As for the night, I spent it in the only room the inn could offer us, and he slept in the car. But you haven't answered my question, Princess.'

'Which was?'

'As to why Signor Vidal cares so little about possible scandal, while his friends seem to care so much.'

With a lifted forefinger, Princess Lagna signalled for her bill. 'I can think of two reasons, neither of which you may like,' she said.

'All the same, I ought to hear them.'

121

'As you wish. The first is that one recognises that Cesare Vidal is the type of man who must have feminine company about him; his regard of himself demands it, and he is not always particular where he looks to find it. And the second—arising from the first—is that he may rate your reputation as being of little concern to him. For instance, where he would not dream of putting mine in jeopardy by sharing his house with me, he may not feel at all the same about yours. You—see?'

Dinah felt the colour drain from her face with anger. 'I see,' she said.

The Princess was looking in a gold mesh purse for money. 'And another thing——'

'Yes?' Dinah was standing now.

'It is that I do wonder why your own *fidanzato* tolerates so false a position for you. For I understand from Cesare that you have one, an Englishman, a colleague. Isn't it so?'

Dinah ignored the question. 'And you say this is why you invited me to tea with you this afternoon?' she asked.

'To see you alone, yes.'

'Then don't let me be under any obligation to you, Princess,' said Dinah. 'For my *tea*,' she added as she took some lire notes from her bag, slapped them down on to the table and stalked away, lips compressed, head high.

Tempted as she was to go straight back to the Palazzo, pack her things, wash her hands of the whole circumstances and move out, a later, cooler sense persuaded her against it.

She guessed that Cesare would not hear from the Princess about her interference in his affairs, and if she hoped to shame Dinah herself into retreat, then she was not going to succeed! Silence and contempt of her malice were the only weapon Dinah had, and though her enemy wouldn't recognise them as weapons, they did something for Dinah's pride.

But she was to be badly dismayed when she learned that Trevor was thinking along the same lines. When she had first told him she was accepting Cesare's offer he had sounded only surprised and slightly affronted that, having promised Etta she would consider the room in the Rio Paglia, she should turn it down in favour of staying where she was. His only comment then had been, 'I'm afraid Etta is going to be hurt, but I suppose the Palazzo d'Orio *is* a grander address than the Rio Paglia, if you care about that sort of thing.' But when she had ignored the sourness of that. he hadn't made her justify her yielding to Cesare's persuasion, and she thought he had accepted it until, a day or two after the Princess's attack, he demanded suddenly,

'When is Signora Vidal supposed to be coming home?'

The inconsequence of the question took Dinah aback. 'When? she echoed. 'Oh, very soon now, I think. Why?'

As soon as she had spoken she had guessed at the drift of his thought, and she was right.

He said tautly, 'Because I understood you were only putting in time until she did return. But it's been more than a fortnight now, and you couldn't have expected it would be so long when you agreed with Cesare Vidal to stay. He must have told you a date, or——'

'He didn't,' said Dinah. ' "Very soon now" or "Shortly" was what he said.'

'And you accepted that?'

'Yes.'

'And so did I, when you told me. But I never thought, as you couldn't have done, that it would be for more than a weekend or a few days at most.'

Put on the defensive and not liking it, 'Well, I didn't make a time-check, I'm afraid. Was that wrong?' she queried.

'It was pretty indiscreet, wasn't it, agreeing to live alone in the house with the man for some vague time of his choosing?' Trevor retorted.

'Indiscreet?' (This was the Gritti Palace confrontation all over again!) 'Yes, perhaps,' she agreed. '*If* we were alone in the house without two other people always there, and *if* I were more than a lodger, seeing my landlord at most once a day and not always that. And if——'

'All right, you needn't go on,' Trevor interrupted her.' But you can't brush off the situation as airily as that. It's going to make for some unpleasant gossip, and you could consider the position in which it puts me, even if you are deliberately blind to what could be said about yourself.'

'You—in what position, and with whom?'

'Why, where I'd need to find excuses for you, explanations. And with anyone who knows us both; knows where we stand with each other, of course.'

124

Dinah said slowly, 'But do you know, Trevor, that I'm not at all sure of that myself? I haven't been for a long time, and I doubt if you have either.'

He stared. 'Not sure—about us? But you're my girl, aren't you?'

Touched, 'Am I?' she appealed.

'Well, I'd always assumed so. We've known each other, worked in the same job, gone about together for—well, for how long now?'

The moment of softness passed, she longed to retort, *For too long now, without making any plans, without any deep-felt love. Without belonging.* Instead she said aloud,

'For long enough, you think, to entitle you to warn me against a nasty situation which I assure you, expecting you to believe me, that I'm not really in?'

Trevor said, '*I'm* ready enough to believe you think you're in no danger from gossip or scandal. Because if you ever had thought so, you wouldn't have invited it so brazenly. But the man I don't trust not to make the most of his opportunities with you is Cesare Vidal. And you can like that or not, as you please.'

'Assuming, I take it, that, having chosen his opportunity to make me some improper advances, I wouldn't have enough dignity of my own to resist?'

'Frankly, considering his reputation for—technique with women, no. Which is why——' Trevor hesitated, bit his lip, swallowed hard and repeated himself—'Which is why I've decided to ask you to marry me. As soon as it's possible. To—to protect you from him.'

CHAPTER SEVEN

From the look on Trevor's face Dinah sensed that hearing himself make his proposal had surprised him as much as it had startled her.

After a moment she said gently, 'I don't think you meant that seriously, did you? You don't want to marry me quite soon, or even in any forseeable time. It hasn't been in your mind.'

'Should I have asked you if I hadn't meant it?' he asked roughly.

'I think you might have done on your impulse to protect me from Cesare—a protection which I assure you I don't need.'

'I'd have thought it showed I care what happens to you!'

Dinah nodded. 'So it does, and I'm grateful. But that isn't enough to marry on. You could care about me in that way if you were my brother.'

'Then what *would* you consider "enough"?'

She sighed. 'Something—some feeling—I doubt if we've ever felt for each other.'

'You are talking about passion? Sex?' Trevor questioned.

'Including them. But more, I think on my side, a need to share all of myself with you, to give you everything, to hold nothing back.'

126

'I'd never ask that of you!' he denied.

'I know you wouldn't. But I feel I ought to *want* to give it, and that you ought to want to give it to me. Less than that isn't love.'

'But we share a lot as it is! Our work, for one thing.'

'Which we could share with a good friend—another man for you, a woman friend for me.'

'Not in the same way—with an eye to the future. You must know I don't want to marry until I'm more established in my career,' he accused.

She saw a flaw in his argument. 'Yes,' she said. 'I have known. I do know. And that's why I wouldn't have the right to take you up on the—the generous offer you've just made me for a not-good-enough reason for your making it——' She broke off. 'Oh, Trevor my dear, don't you see that if we did love each other enough, we shouldn't be arguing this out? We'd be in each other's arms!'

When he ignored her tentatively outstretched hand, she knew she was right, though she wouldn't make a triumph of it. He said dully, 'Then that's that I suppose. We've come to the end of the road. You're refusing me after all this time?'

'Yes. It wouldn't be fair or right for either of us, though it probably had to take all this time to find it out. But, Trevor——'

'Yes?'

Dinah had needed her moment of pause to decide whether she could betray Etta's confidence. But she had only given her word to the girl when they had

127

both thought Trevor was committed to herself, and so she went on.

'You know, there *is* someone who, I'm sure, does feel that "enough" for you that I don't. It's Etta. Hadn't you guessed?'

'*Etta?* How do you know?'

Dinah noticed he hadn't denied the possibility. 'Because she told me so weeks ago, while she believed you had hardly even noticed her. Don't you remember how her work fell off, and you didn't know why?'

'What had that to do with it?'

'Everything. She so desperately wanted to be all-in-all to you that she tried too hard to please you, and when she failed, every criticism you had to make of her cut deep.'

Trevor said thoughtfully, 'She was much better after you talked to her. Was that why?'

'I hope so. I told her I knew you valued her work, and that the way to make you value her in other ways was to do that well, at least.'

'So you didn't care even then if I came to value her more than I valued you? You knew *then*?'

Dinah shook her head. 'Not for certain. But I suspected that before long we might both know that marriage wasn't for us. And I think we're agreed about it, aren't we?'

'I don't know. You've sprung it on me. You can't expect me to be glad. Etta——' He turned away.

'Be kind to her, Trevor,' Dinah urged.

'I am kind to her. I'm very fond of her.'

128

'Then be kinder still. You'll find it rewarding,' Dinah said to his back.

It took some will for her to admit that she had let Cesare persuade her too easily of his mother's imminent homecoming. She hadn't wanted to know a definite date, but the combined attacks of the Princess and of Trevor put a limit to her complacency, and on the next evening when he did dine at home with her, she put the question to him again.

'She should have been here by now,' he said.

'Should she?' (So he hadn't deliberately deceived her.)

'If she hadn't suddenly decided to take a visit to her sister in England on her way. I only heard this morning. She telephoned my office. She's there now.'

'With Mrs Herbert? Then she will see the twins, I expect,' said Dinah.

'That,' he said, 'was the object of the exercise, I gather. She wanted to make up to them for not having been here when, as she said in her best American, they "stopped by".'

Dinah laughed. 'That was generous of her, considering how they "stopped by" uninvited. But neither of them will be at home now. They're both training.'

'Which, if I know my mother, won't prevent her from commanding their presence whenever she orders it. However, her current plans are that she will be flying in at the end of next week.' He paused. 'I hope you aren't going to efface yourself quite so thoroughly when she does arrive?'

129

Dinah flushed. 'I haven't thought that your inviting me to stay on has entitled me to intrude on you when you have guests.'

'As I'm your host, mightn't you allow me to decide whether or not you would be intruding? Anyway, where have you been when you've gone out?'

Trust him to have no delicate scruples against asking anything he wanted to know! thought Dinah. 'I've tried various restaurants for an evening meal, and sometimes I go to the cinema,' she told him.

His brows lifted. 'Alone?'

'Yes.'

'No escorting Englishman?'

'If you mean Trevor Land, he has to study for a Management course in the evenings.' She didn't know what prompted her to add, 'Besides, I haven't the right any longer to such spare time as he does have.'

'No? Since when?'

'He asked me to marry him the other day, and I refused.'

Cesare's long look studied her. 'You said No to him? But when I attempted a few random moonlight kisses, you put me in the wrong for assuming you weren't already committed to the man!'

'Yes, well—I thought I might be, then.'

'So why didn't his proposal clinch it?'

'Because I know he doesn't love me.'

'Then why should he commit himself to marriage with you?'

She couldn't report Trevor's reluctantly chivalrous, 'To protect you from Cesare Vidal.' She said instead, 'I think he had got used to the idea of me; used to

130

going about with me; having me around, and it isn't enough.'

'Though by his reckoning, mightn't that add up to loving you in his fashion?'

She shook her head. 'Not with him. I've been just part of the furnishing of his scene. Besides, a woman always knows when she is loved.'

'Does she? Always? I'd doubt that very much,' said Cesare. 'You could go on hoping.'

It wasn't until she was alone that, aghast, she realised the import of that. She knew now she had told Cesare about Trevor's proposal because she had wanted to put the record straight about herself and Trevor. So what had she said, or rather, failed to say, which had left him thinking that, on her side, she was in love with Trevor; was still 'hoping'?

Instead of telling Cesare that she knew Trevor didn't love her, it would have been so easy to say, 'We don't love each other enough.' So why, by some quirk of thought or intention, hadn't she said it? Mentally, she rehearsed ways of bringing up the subject again; ways of telling Cesare that Trevor meant no more to her than she did to him. But even in rehearsal all the words sounded too bald, too pointed. And anyway, as she remembered she had thought before, what did it matter to Cesare whether she had hopes of a future with Trevor—or hadn't? It had only been his innate need to analyse people's motives —which perhaps lent him power with them—that had wanted to know.

The next time he had friends to dinner at the Palazzo he rather unnecessarily asked if she were free to join them, and of course she was.

'Don't dress,' he said. 'The men are only business cronies, but one of them who is married, Enrico Rienzi, will bring his wife, who always complains if she hasn't another woman for company while we talk shop. So will you come?'

Dinah was relieved that that sounded as if Francia Lagna would not be there. She didn't quite know how to interpret 'Don't dress', so she chose black-and-white—a sunray pleated skirt with a creamy deep-cuffed silk shirt worn above a belt of black and white plaited leather. Signora Rienzi, ('call me Carla'), a plump young woman in her early thirties, was in even less formal dress of a pink linen trouser suit and clump-heeled sandals on bare feet.

'You see what I mean?' she demanded plaintively of Dinah when the men, all of them connected with films, went through the minimum of social attentions over the aperitifs, before plunging into the deeps of technical jargon and problems over dinner. 'Enrico says to me, "Why do you come with me to business meals? If you do not like to hear me arranging our good future, why do you not go to bed with a book?" But I say to him, "And is then our marriage, not yet a year old, an affair of my bed alone with a *book*?" So I come with him, though I am always bored, and in return I insist he takes me somewhere gay and expensive on at least one night a week. Which he does, knowing how I can sulk when I am not pleased,' she concluded with some satisfaction.

Dinah did see what she meant. The men's talk was almost beyond any lay understanding, and they

132

barely acknowledged Dinah's and Signora Rienzi's leaving the table at the end of dinner by rising perfunctorily from their chairs before resuming whatever argument was then in progress.

Over coffee in the *salotto* Carla Rienzi jerked her head in the direction of the dining-room. 'They are at odds, those others, over more than their camera angles and their projections and their lightings,' she told Dinah. 'One of the bones they tear between them is the matter of Francia Lagna—the Principessa Lagna. You have met her, of course?'

On Dinah's saying she had, Carla went on, 'Enrico will not have it that she can act. Bernini says, "She has a beautiful face and body, but——" I think Pedro Luiz is neutral. It is Sorensen, the Swede, and Cesare who believe in her talent and insist she must be developed and groomed at all costs.'

Dinah nodded, 'Yes, Signor Vidal told me once he thought she was bound for stardom. But she hasn't been in any films yet, has she?'

'No. They count on her title and her looks to launch her in the big way. Sorensen wants to take her to Sweden or at least to Rome. But she has her own reasons for remaining in Venice—and her hopes of Cesare not the least of them, one hears.'

'Is her home here in Venice?' Dinah asked.

'Oh no. She is Sicilian, and a princess only by outworn title, not by wealth. She stays now with a rich uncle, a retired silk merchant who has a villa on the banks of the Brenta, and of course it would do much for her own fortunes if she could capture Cesare Vidal, whether or not she ever makes the film scene.

Myself, I think she feels she would do better by going with Sorensen. But he is married and loves his wife. And two stones to one bird is a poor bargain——' Carla Rienzi stopped and giggled. 'Do you not express it the other way about—one stone to two birds? Marriage with Cesare *and* film stardom!'

Dinah's wishful thinking could not resist the comment, 'How hopeful is she that he will ask her to marry him?'

Carla shrugged. 'As hopeful, one supposes, as any of us can afford to be when we have chosen the man we want. If we are clever, we get; if we are too clever or not clever at all, we do not. But I should think Francia Lagna will not make many mistakes.'

'She is certainly very beautiful and poised,' Dinah's honesty conceded.

'And very sure of her success with men Which makes one wonder why she resents even the most ordinary of females who cross her path. Secretaries, file clerks, continuity girls, all of them harmless enough. But she greets them all with the arched back and wreathing neck of a pussy-cat on guard.' Carla paused to consider Dinah thoughtfully. 'Considering your position here in Cesare's house, *signorina*, it is more wonder still that she tolerates you!'

'Well, we have met very seldom, and she probably appreciates that Signor Vidal asked me to stay after I was burned out of my rented apartment,' said Dinah, giving nothing away.

'Or, more likely, Cesare has dared her to suppose there is anything to suspect of your relationship, and she knows better than to cross him by appearing to think otherwise,' replied Carla, evidently to her own satisfaction, since, to Dinah's relief, she pursued the subject no further.

That was the first of two dinner-parties to which Cesare invited Dinah that week. On the second evening the Princess was among his guests, as were the wives of two of the men who were there. A third man came alone, and was partnered with Dinah at the dinner-table.

At that party the men were more attentive to the ladies, possibly because there were more of them, possibly because, in any mixed company, Princess Lagna was the kind of woman who would never be ignored. But in the main it was a dinner of business associates, and much of the talk was of business matters.

The men, it appeared, were interested in buying a chain of small tourist hotels which was about to come on to the market. In the course of the discussion someone suggested that as some of them had lost reputation lately, the price asked for the chain might be very attractive.

'Reputation for what? Service? Cleanliness? The menus? What?' It was Cesare who put the question.

'I don't know the details. It's just a word that is going round. And it doesn't apply to all of them,' the other man said.

'Which, then?'

The man named four of the seven establishments involved. Of the four Dinah recognised two as middle-priced hotels to which Plenair sometimes sent clients. The man went on, 'If it's true, and the chain goes to auction, it could keep the bidding favourably low.'

'And it could work the other way. If the standards have dropped too far, having bought, we could find ourselves with no bargain at all,' put in another of the guests.

'We should only move on the results of confidential reports, of course,' said Cesare.

'Professional reports?'

'Of the premises and so on, yes. But it occurs to me that for the really valuable and honest assessment, we could do worse than look to the actual users of the places—the ordinary clients.'

The first man laughed. 'And how do you propose to get those, *amico mio*?' he queried. 'Station yourself in the foyer with a clip-board of questions—"*Per favore, signore, signora*, how have you dined tonight? How have you been served?" You would be popular with the management, I must say!'

Cesare laughed easily with him, but his own wife scolded, 'Do not exaggerate, Bertholde! Cesare is right. It is we, the customers, who know best what is service and what is food, and know which place we shall not patronise again, and others where we shall return.'

'Except,' Princess Lagna was heard to murmur, 'that neither Cesare, nor you, Signora Lesogno, nor any of us would be likely ever to visit hotels of the level of those we have been discussing, much less to go back to them later?'

Signora Lesogno turned on her. 'Speak for yourself, Princess,' she advised tartly. 'These places are all of good, medium standard. If they were not, our syndicate wouldn't be interested in adding them to its other properties.' She turned back to Cesare. 'You have a good idea there,' she told him. 'And how do you carry it out? You send into each of the places where you suspect the service is not all it should be —someone whom you can trust to report fairly on them, and you act on what he tells you about them, good or bad.'

Cesare said, 'The honest judgment of an ordinary client, h'm?'

'Exactly.'

Cesare looked round the table. 'I think Clara may have something, gentlemen. What do you say?'

There was a murmur of assent, and Cesare went on, 'Then we send someone in, as Clara suggests. It shouldn't be too difficult to find a suitable man for the job.'

'Or a woman.'

They all looked at Signora Lesogno, who repeated, 'That is what I said—a woman. And in every case, a woman alone. For that is the test of the attitude of any management towards its clients—the way in which it treats any woman of ordinary appearance without an escort. Isn't that so?' she appealed to the other women, two of whom nodded agreement, while Princess Lagna murmured, 'I really don't know that I have ever had the experience——'

'I said, "of ordinary appearance",' Clara Lesogno reminded her. 'By which I meant—a little shy-mannered, not readily noticed, lacking the glamour

137

which would have any staff falling over themselves to serve her, escorted or not.'

'Oh——' said Francia, sitting back and making the monosyllable express her satisfaction that no one expected her to have had the experience of dining alone, unremarked. And the other woman went on, 'So you see it calls for a woman, not a regular client of any of these places, but one who would not look out of place to their particular class of custom. Preferably of the tourist type they cater for. A foreigner, perhaps. But one who understands our language well enough to appreciate whether she is being well or disgracefully treated. You see?'

With thoughtful nods the company indicated that it 'saw', and Bertholde Lesogno looked his approval of his wife's shrewd grasp of the situation. It was Francia who said to Cesare, 'You know, it seems to me that if you take up Clara's suggestion, you haven't any problem. Of someone suitable for your purpose, I mean. For here, at your own table, you have the very girl——' her brilliant glance went to Dinah and back again. 'She doesn't dress flashily; she speaks and understands our language well; from her job, she must know what service to expect of any hotel, and she should fit in with the clientele of these places without any difficulty at all!'

Cesare said, 'You mean—Dinah?'

The Princess nodded smiling assent.

Cesare looked at the other men. 'It's a thought,' he said, and turned to Dinah. 'And what does Dinah say?'

Dinah hesitated. By anyone other than Francia she

138

might have felt complimented. But as things were between them, she found that lady's enthusiasm suspect and full of hidden barbs. At last she said to Cesare, 'I don't quite know. It depends on what you would want of me; what I should have to do?'

'Of course,' he agreed, and then, 'We'll talk about it later, if we may.' His glance went to Signora Lesogno, the senior lady there. Reading the signal in his look, she rose; the other women followed her lead and they went out of the room, leaving the men at the table.

Later, in the *salotto*, Cesare drew Dinah aside.

'We've given Clara's suggestion the works, and if you would co-operate with us, we'd be grateful,' he said. 'It shouldn't prove very onerous, I think—very little more than you've been doing voluntarily for some time, in order, you said, not to incommode me.'

'Dining out alone, you mean?'

'Or lunching, though dining would be preferable, as a girl alone in the evening is more vulnerable to neglect by staff, if any is intended. And making a report afterwards on your experience at each place, that's all.'

'Would you want me to stay the night?'

'We discussed that, but I think not, unless you can't get a clear picture by spending an evening and dining by yourself. Would you mind going to the bar alone?'

She smiled wryly. 'I don't do so usually, and I shouldn't much care to.'

'Then don't,' advised Cesare, just as the Princess came within earshot and paused by his side. 'Are you

139

briefing Dinah for her mission?' she asked archly.

'We were just agreeing that it shouldn't be necessary for her to run the gauntlet of the hotel bars, which she might find embarrassing.'

'Oh, but'—the brilliant eyes widened—'surely that is where she could best learn just how embarrassed some hotels could make a homely kind of spinster feel?'

'Though weren't you claiming at dinner that you had no experience whatsoever of how a lone woman could be treated?' Cesare challenged indulgently.

The Princess's finger and thumb flicked his sleeve coquettishly. (In an eighteenth-century drawing-room she would have used her fan just so, thought Dinah.) 'You! You have too good a memory!' she chided him. 'But do you think that, even without the experience, I have no imagination either? Could I act —as you tell me I can—if I couldn't get into the skin of people less sheltered than I seem always to be?' She turned to Dinah with a smile which went no further than her lips. 'So *brave* of you, I think, to take this on! Or do you perhaps feel that you owe Cesare too much to be able to refuse him?' she purred.

Not returning the smile, Dinah looked straight at Cesare. 'Yes, perhaps that's it. I do owe him a great deal,' she said.

She kept her first assignment at one of the seven hotels of the chain the following evening. When she returned to the Palazzo she told Cesare she had found nothing to criticise. The atmosphere of the place was welcoming, the menu excellently varied and she had been attentively served. Afterwards, in her role as wallflower, she had gone alone to the dance-floor, where the master of ceremonies had introduced her to a most correct young man who had seen her to her *motoscafo* when she had wanted to leave.

On her second excursion, to one of the four of which there had been earlier complaints, she was less fortunate. At her third, to one of the places recommended by Plenair, she was as well received as at the first. There she had gone rather late; people were leaving, rather than arriving, and across the dining-room as she took the seat the waiter held for her, she saw Trevor with Etta on their way out.

Dinah smiled to herself, having no pangs, no regrets. 'Thank goodness he doesn't seem to regard Etta as "junior staff" whom he can't afford to be seen escorting!' she thought, and wondered whether, or how soon, she might expect Etta to confide progress to her.

Since she had been promoted to handling Day Tours she had been less in the office, and in consequence had seen less of both Trevor and Etta. But the next day a glowing Etta waylaid her in the cloak-room.

'Lately I haven't liked to stop you to talk to you,' the girl confessed. 'You always seem to be on your way somewhere, but I really have wanted you to know how sorry I was about you and—and Trevor.' Trevor.'

Dinah smiled. 'You needn't be,' she said. 'Our break-up was mutual, and I'd told you, hadn't I, that

141

I was sure neither of us was convinced that we wanted to marry?'

'Yes, but——'

'Well, it had to come out into the open some time, and after it had, I couldn't be as glad as I am about you and Trevor if I had loved him or if he had really loved me.'

Etta blushed. 'Then you know about us? I was dreading having to tell you.'

'Let's say I've hoped,' said Dinah. 'You had told me how *you* felt, and I've hoped that he would come to it as soon as he admitted to himself that he hadn't ever loved me. So I'm sure he isn't just on the re-bound from me. He's all yours!'

'I begin to think so,' Etta agreed happily. 'Working together as we do, we have so much to talk about. In fact, we hardly ever stop, even out of office hours. He takes me about a lot; we picnic at weekends, and he has been home with me, and once a week we have dinner at an hotel——'

'Yes, I saw you last night—at the Regale,' put in Dinah.

'You did? We didn't see you there with anyone.'

'I was alone and rather late, and you were just leaving, looking totally engrossed with each other. So wrapped up that I wouldn't have dared to call out "Hi!" ' Dinah laughed.

'But you could have dared. You, of all people, could,' Etta assured her earnestly. 'Because if Trevor does love me—and he says he does and—and shows it, I think, it will be you who will have helped to work the magic.'

'Not me,' Dinah denied stoutly. 'Whatever magic there may have been around, you've worked it for yourselves.' She looked at her watch. 'I must go.'

'There you are! You are just as taken up with your work as Trevor is,' commented Etta. 'He is always saying "I must go——" and he goes. But I love him for it, and just as long as he always comes back——!' She left a contented little sigh on the air.

On the evening when Signora Vidal was due to fly in from London, Cesare surprised Dinah by inviting her to go over with him to the airport to meet her. They went in the launch, its luggage space cleared of everything which might impede the mountain of excess baggage which Cesare said he expected his mother to have.

She had. The piled-high porter's trolley which preceded her into the reception hall she waved towards the landing-quay with an exquisitely-gloved hand while she herself made a direct line towards her son.

She was tall, slim in a lavender trouser suit, silver-blue hair curling from under a silk scarf draped and knotted turbanwise. She wore the minimum of make-up on her deeply bronzed skin; her eyes were a clear English blue, creased at their corners by laughter-lines; there was a lift to her mouth which matched Cesare's. Everything about her—clothes, cosmetics, poise—made her fully the contemporary of her much younger half-sister, the twins' mother. Well into her fifties, Ursula Vidal had come to terms with both middle age and widowhood. She was very much her own woman.

She acknowledged Dinah with a smile—'You are

Dinah—nice girl!' and slinging her handbag up her arm, held Cesare off by a grip on both his elbows.

'And how many marinas have you planned, how many gondola-ranks have you taken over, how many Old Masters have you bought for investment, and how many girls have you made love to and forgotten while I've been away?' she teased him.

He detached himself and in his turn held her off before he kissed her.

'You'd be surprised, Mamma, how few of any of them. My technique must be slipping,' he said.

CHAPTER EIGHT

To Dinah's relief, Signora Vidal saw nothing questionable in her return to the Palazzo after the fire. 'I should not have forgiven Cesare if he hadn't insisted on your coming back,' she declared. 'But Jason and Lesley tell me you may not be staying in Venice after the end of your season. What about that?'

'It depends,' Dinah told her, 'on whether I'm asked to stay on for some clerical work—the spring bookings and so on. I should like to stay, but I shan't know about it for a week or two, and of course if I do stay, I shall find a new apartment for myself. In fact, I've begun looking for one.'

'Nonsense, child. There's no hurry. I need young people about me. That's why I was so sorry to have missed the twins, and who knows how long I may have to wait for grandchildren while Cesare doesn't marry?'

'I'm glad you were able to see the twins,' said Dinah. 'Did you manage it more than once?'

'Oh yes. They were both able to get home for a weekend and when they weren't free I went to Reading and to Oxford and took them each out to luncheon separately. I've arranged for them to come out again for Christmas. Jason has a vacation from his college, but Lesley will have to wangle time off from her nursing.' The Signora stopped to laugh.

' "Wangle"! That puts me in my generation, doesn't it?'

Dinah laughed with her. Since the Signora had come home they all spoke English—overlaid by Americanisms from the Signora and Italian for emphasis when she needed it.

'I expect you met my people too?' Dinah asked.

'I did indeed. I found your mother a poppet and your father a reminder of my own. They miss you sadly, but I told them they mustn't expect you home too soon—we must make you a real Venetian first; get the very feel of the city into your blood, as it got into mine when Cesare's father and I were falling in love. But you'll have heard all about that?'

'Yes. Cesare told the twins when they wanted to know——'

The Signora waited as Dinah paused. 'Wanted to know what?' she prompted.

'Nothing. That is——'

The Signora waited again. 'Well?'

Dinah saw she had to make the best of her *gaffe.* 'It was when Jason read aloud your first letter to them and they asked Cesare what you meant by your joke of—of warning him against me. He knew you were only joking, of course, but that was when he told us about you and Signor Vidal.'

Cesare's mother threw back her head and laughed. 'Joke? I meant it as a true parallel of what could happen!' she declared. 'But even if you and Cesare haven't converged, as Claudio and I did, almost at sight, like a couple of colliding planets, I hope he has been gallant enough- to take you about—to the theatre, nightclubs, dining out and so on?'

Dinah said, 'He has asked me to meet some of his friends here at dinner, but he is always very busy and he has a lot of engagements of his own, as I've had mine.'

'Well, he must take us both out one evening,' decided his mother. 'To celebrate my homecoming will make as good a reason as any.'

But when the arranged evening came she pleaded a headache. She would go to bed with a sedative and hot milk, ruling that Cesare must take Dinah out all the same.

'Please not—we could go another time just as well, Dinah urged, and enlisted Cesare's support. 'Couldn't we?'

'Of course,' he agreed. But his mother was firm. 'You will have put off other engagements to keep this one with us, I've no doubt, and Dinah will have been looking forward to it. An empty evening for you both, with nothing to do with it but watch television, just because of me? Besides, Tomasa is not expecting to have to serve dinner and will be none too pleased if she must. No, you will take yourselves out as we arranged, and I shall go to bed. It is settled.'

'Just because, in these days, the domestic staff must be placated? Really, Mamma, I didn't think you could be so craven!' Cesare chided her, but added to Dinah, 'Our home despot has spoken—we play it as a duet instead of a trio.'

Dinah was glad he couldn't guess at the excited sense of occasion with which she dressed for the evening, her first in 'duet' with him since the night when his impulse had taken her out on the lagoon by moonlight—a memory which could still send a shiver of thrill down her spine. When he handed her into the launch where Giuseppe was at the wheel she looked up and back at him, smiling.

'This is a unique experience for me,' she said.

He took the seat beside her, signalling Giuseppe to move off. 'Unique? How so?' he asked.

'It's the only time I've been taken out to dinner by water—chauffeur-driven.'

'But you'll have been escorted for the evening dozens of times since you came to Venice?'

'Sometimes, but by water-taxi or on foot. It isn't the same, and it could only happen in Venice.'

'I daresay your own Thames could oblige in much the same way, if your escort laid it on,' Cesare suggested.

She shook her head. 'Don't spoil the image for me. I *want* it to be able to happen only in Venice.'

'Why should you?'

'Because, after I've left it, I want to remember Venice as unique.'

'Which it is. When are you thinking of leaving?'

'I don't know. It depends,' she answered him as she had answered his mother, though he didn't ask her to enlarge on why she might stay.

He was taking her to the exclusive Casa La Corba, and when they moored at its private quay he told Giuseppe to come back for them at midnight. 'After dinner we can dance here, if you'd care to,' he told Dinah as the doorman bowed them in to the foyer.

This will only happen once. I must remember it

148

all, Dinah thought, looking about her at the dining-room, the décor of which was boldly maritime. Over-head, fishing-nets draped a canopy; ancient amphorae were wired to the pillars; the wall frescoes were of brilliantly coloured tropical fish and the subdued lighting was by ships' lanterns. She asked Cesare to choose a menu for her and they ate a shell fish salad, veal stuffed with truffles, and drank a fine Chianti. Cesare seemed to know and be known by a great many of the restaurant's patrons, and they had reached the dessert course when the Swede whom Dinah had met once at the Palazzo came over to speak to Cesare.

He bowed to Dinah and excused his taking Cesare a little aside. They talked for a few minutes and when Cesare returned to the table he said, 'We are taking Francia Lagna to Stockholm for film tests shortly. Sorensen wanted to tell me it is all arranged with the Swedish studio he has in mind for her début.'

Dinah remembered Carla Rienzi's gossip about the Princess's future, and did not care much for the sound of Cesare's "we".'

'*You* are taking her?' she asked.

'With Sorensen as her co-sponsor. He sees in her the makings of a very valuable property and wants to ensure she has all the support she deserves.'

Half wishing she could ask, 'And how do *you* see her?' Dinah knew she didn't really want to hear Cesare's answer. If he told her the truth, that was, and didn't tease her with one of his cryptic evasions. *He* considered he was entitled to a straight answer to any question he cared to put. But she didn't come

149

in the same mould of assurance and she knew she would be depressed by whatever he said. With his first mention of the Princess's name, the evening of which she had meant to make an enchanted memory had begun to fall apart for Dinah. Yet outwardly nothing had changed. She would continue to be as pleasant a dinner companion as she could. And for him the evening would be—just another evening!

After dinner they danced once or twice on the tiny floor, and at eleven there was a display of Latin-American dancing. Afterwards the professional dancers mingled with the guests and Dinah found herself invited on to the floor by a sinuous young man in a black cat-suit who, after one round of the floor, flattered her by telling her she was a 'natural', and though she was under no illusion that he did not say the same thing to each of his amateur partners, she still allowed him to persuade her to a second tango after the first.

During that one he looked beyond her shoulder and murmured. 'I must not keep you after this dance, *signora*. Your husband does not look pleased.'

'My—husband?'

'From whom I asked permission for one dance with you—not more. And he is a jealous man— yes?'

'Oh!' Dinah found her wits. 'My dinner partner? But he is not my husband. Just a friend.'

'Yet still with a right to be jealous of you in the arms of another man? Ah well'—the seemingly boneless shoulders shrugged—'we had better make *fiale, signora*—so!' And catching her closely to his lithe body he executed with her a series of swift but beautifully controlled gyrations which brought them up short and accurately at Cesare's table.

He murmured, '*Grazie, signora*', made an elaborate gesture of kissing Dinah's hand and bowed himself away. Wondering what he had read as jealousy in Cesare's face and thinking she would have been gratified to detect it too, she sat down, panting a little. Cesare said, 'From your look of rapture I gather you'll be marking that down as a unique experience too? You both seemed intent on giving an almost exhibition performance. Why did you cut it short?'

Since she couldn't tell him why, she scoffed, 'Exhibition? Unique? It was just different, that was all. I didn't seem to be doing any of the steps by my own volition, but by his.'

'The professional touch.' Cesare looked at his watch. 'However, if there's not too much difference between the sublime and the ridiculous, would you care to dance again with me before we leave?'

She went eagerly into his arms, knowing there a difference at which he would never guess—warmth and feeling and longing, against a cool expertise which had made her perform like a puppet, directed by the pulling of a string. Even if Cesare had really been in love with her, how could he have shown jealousy of that?

They went out into a gentle night air. Giuseppe was ready with the launch, but Cesare paused on the quay. 'It's warm. Shall we walk home instead?' he asked.

'Yes, please.' Dinah liked the intimate sound of

'home'—a place shared with him for however short a time now.

'Very well.' He dismissed Giuseppe and the launch and took her intimately by the arm, matching his stride to hers.

Walking so, they were very close, hip touching hip occasionally, her long skirts brushing against his leg. Looking up at the brilliancy of stars against their dark backcloth of sky, he observed, 'No waxing moon tonight, so you're in no danger of unprovoked assault,' and then, without giving her a chance to reply to the deliberate challenge of that, he went on to ask casually whether Signora Vidal had yet invited her to her dower house.

'I didn't know she had one,' Dinah said. 'You mean, she won't be staying on at the Palazzo when—when the time comes?'

'No. She is English enough to crave a garden, and when I marry she plans to move to a little villa among all the big ones on the banks of the Brenta, where there is a garden and where, she says, she looks forward to seeing her grandchildren play. I'm surprised she hasn't shown you over it by now.'

Though Dinah couldn't think of any reason why Signora Vidal should have done so, she said merely, 'She may not realise how much any of our sex enjoys looking over empty houses, and besides, I'm working all day. There wouldn't have been a lot of time.'

'Which wouldn't deter Mother, who can usually make her own time and organise other people's for anything she wants to do. Besides, there are always Sundays,' Cesare replied.

It was to seem that Signora Vidal had had the same thought, for the following Sunday her invitation to Dinah was tantamount to a royal command.

'Cesare has engagements, so Giuseppe will take us by the launch to the Piazzale Roma, where we shall take a taxi for the river road,' she announced. 'My villa is cleaned and kept in order by a village woman, whom I have asked to prepare a cold luncheon which we will eat on the garden-terrace, and afterwards you shall advise me on the planning of my garden.'

'Advice which you must not expect Mamma to take,' Cesare commented drily to Dinah. 'It is counsel which she demands from all her friends without, I suspect, the slightest intention of using it.'

'But it pleases people to be asked, and it is only by tapping the opinion of others that one learns which mistakes not to make. Isn't that so?' his mother appealed.

'It certainly has the virtue that, when you finally go your own way and take the wrong one, you'll have no one but yourself to blame,' he allowed.

'Exactly,' the Signora nodded agreement. 'And if I may say so, it happens to be an attitude which I've learned from you.'

'Does it?'

'You should know, son,' she retorted crisply. 'For when did you ever fail to demand to be given your head in anything you had decided to do?'

His reply was a shrug. 'As long as we are agreed we are two of a kind, Dinah has been warned,' he said, and left it there.

After their taxi had crossed the modern causeway

153

to the mainland, it abandoned the autostrada for the older road to Padua which ran, at first intermittently and then continually, along the river bank. It was a district of luxurious villas, some of the older ones past their earlier glories as the homes of rich Venetian merchants, others renovated and modernised, with swimming pools in their grounds and sailing yachts at their mooring-stages.

Signora Vidal indicated one of the latter to Dinah. 'The Villa Bacardi, where Francia Lagna stays with her uncle,' she said. 'My little *casa* is much more humble. *Le Rose*, I call it.'

Le Rose, well named for the riot of late-showing yellow roses which covered its façade, was a little square white house surrounded by a terraced garden stepping down to the river frontage, where a pair of swans lazed on the sun-warmed water. As far as Dinah could judge, the garden was already planned —there was not much to be done with its slopes but to keep its cut terraces as they were. But she could picture them massed in the spring with rock flowering plants and in the summer, perhaps, with floribunda roses, and she could appreciate how the place must appeal to someone who was garden-hungry in a city of channelled water and ancient stone and brick, colourful and lovely as they were in their way.

The villa was a doll's house of two rooms downstairs and two up, the latter connected by a bathroom and each with its own tiny sun balcony. Signora Vidal and Dinah lunched on the loggia roofed by plaited bamboo, and afterwards the Signora did go through the motions of asking Dinah's opinion as to what might be best done with both the garden and the furnishing of the house, which at present held only a few well-cared-for antiques.

'I ask myself whether I shall come here next spring, next summer—when?' the Signora mused aloud, and then startled Dinah by demanding, 'Tell me, when do *you* think it might be that Cesare is going to present me with his choice of a bride—take her or leave her, as I may dearly wish to do?'

'I?' Dinah looked her surprise at the question. 'I'm afraid I haven't any idea when he thinks of getting married. He doesn't confide in me.'

'But you have lived as his guest in our house. You must know whom he sees; which of his various girl-friends he takes about most often? Francia Lagna, for instance? How serious would you say he is about her?'

It occurred to Dinah that it was strange for a mother to need to ask such things about her adult son; also that it wasn't quite fair of the Signora to expect to have them answered by a third person. Reluctantly truthful, she said, 'While I have been at the Palazzo, I think he has entertained Princess Lagna more than anyone else, but that may have been for professional reasons, and I don't know how close they may be in—other ways.'

'Tch! You have eyes and ears and a gleam of intuition, one hopes?'

'But not for use on my host's private affairs.'

The Signora laughed. 'The Three Wise Monkeys rolled into one—you!' she chided playfully. 'Very well, I won't pump any more, and we must just hope,

155

mustn't we, that Cesare's motives with regard to Francia Lagna are only professional ones?' After a breath of pause, 'Mustn't we?' she pressed.

Dinah stared again. She knew she had coloured, but refusing to commit herself in words, she queried, 'You mean, *signora*, that you'd prefer to believe Cesare isn't planning to marry the Princess?'

'I mean,' said Cesare's mother, spelling it out, 'that I mostly certainly do *not* want a harpy of a fashion-plate as a daughter-in-law and hoped that you too, as our friend, wouldn't wish to see him waste himself so. However——' with a shrug and a switch to Italian, *'che sarà, sarà*. One cannot fight destiny, after all.'

Which, Dinah thought wryly, was about as phoney a piece of fatalism as she had ever heard. *What will be, will be*, indeed! As if, from all she knew of Cesare Vidal and his mother, either of them would ever yield to the preordained without a fight! As for this issue for or against the Princess Lagna as Cesare's future bride, Dinah was quite sure that, even in mock-resignation, he had never uttered the words *Che sarà, sarà*, and if he meant to marry Francia Lagna, he would.

During that week Dinah finished making the last of her informal reports on the seven hotels, and though she had had some adverse criticisms to make, she was particularly glad that she had been able to praise both those which figured on Plenair's recommended list.

At the outset she had had to argue with Cesare that

156

she was doing the survey voluntarily and for her own interest as much as for his syndicate's purpose. It was pleasant homework which she enjoyed and which widened her experience; therefore no question of payment must be involved.

He curtly demolished this reasoning. 'Nonsense. You are going to places of our choice, not yours, and possibly at times when you might prefer not to go out. Of course you must be paid.'

'For dining out seven times, when you know I often take myself out to a restaurant? And you've said I could choose my own evenings for each one,' she pointed out. 'It's a—a privilege to do it for you. Don't put a price on it, please.'

He appeared to waver. 'At least your expenses?'

She met him half-way. 'Very well. My expenses.'

'Faithfully rendered?'

'To the last single lira,' she had promised him, and had duly added the exact figure to the foot of each report she had made.

She had still found nowhere to live when she would be leaving the Palazzo, and on the day before Cesare and his Swedish colleague were due to fly to Stockholm, Trevor waylaid her and asked her to lunch with him. Surprised by the invitation, she told him she had to be out with a party of tourists all the morning and, accepting, asked him where they should meet. 'At the Grillo as usual?'

'No. At the Casa Savoia on Calle Cervia,' Trevor told her, naming a small restaurant rapidly gaining a name for its cuisine. He had news for her, he said;

in fact, two items, both of which he hoped she would be glad to hear.

When she arrived at the Savoia he was waiting for her in the foyer. He had ordered drinks to be brought to his table, he said, taking her straight into the restaurant where, at the table to which he showed her, Etta was already sitting.

'We're celebrating in a mild way, and we wanted you to be in on it,' Trevor explained Etta's presence. 'Last night we got engaged, and Etta couldn't wait to let you know.'

'Engaged? I'm glad—so *very* glad for you both.' Dinah stooped to kiss the girl's glowing cheek. As she took her seat she teased Trevor, 'A fast worker, you! May I remind you of how short a time ago you were claiming to me that you didn't mean to marry yet?'

'Yes, well'—he had the grace to look abashed —'that was before I'd admitted to myself how much I'd come to value Etta; how little I could bear to let her go, perhaps to another job, perhaps to another fellow. And when she admitted that she felt—something—for me, then we began to go ahead, and very soon it seemed silly to wait, considering how getting married wouldn't interfere with our work at all. Wasn't that how it was, darling?' he appealed to Etta.

She nodded happily. 'Except that it wasn't just work we were concerned with. It was when we realised that we couldn't bear not to share *all* of our life with each other. I think I knew it before Trevor did,' she told Dinah. 'But once he did, that made me happy. And you *are* glad, aren't you?' she appealed wistfully.

'Glad and gratified, both,' Dinah assured her.

'Gratified?'

'Terribly glad for you, and gratified that Trevor and I realised before it was too late that we were only skirmishing on the edge of loving each other enough for marriage——'

'You realised it. I didn't want to,' he put in.

'But you must have agreed in your heart, or you would have rushed me, as you seem to have rushed Etta. You are not getting him merely on the rebound from me, and I'm flattered that you wanted me to be the first one to know,' Dinah told Etta. 'When is the wedding to be?'

'Next month, we thought, when the season will be finished,' said Trevor.

'And you'll invite me, though I don't know yet whether I shall still be here for it?'

'You should be, I think. Just before I asked you to lunch this morning old man Corotti sent a memo through to pass on to you, to see him in his office at ten o'clock tomorrow morning.'

'And you think that means he's going to keep me on?'

'I'd say so, certainly. What else could it mean? And that was the other piece of news I had for you,' Trevor said.

But Dinah was to find that the 'else' which was the purpose of the manager's summons to her was very different from her hopes.

159

He had sent his secretary out of his room and he greeted Dinah curtly from behind his desk, pointing her to a chair.

She sat down. Signor Corotti was not renowned for affability, and she had not expected wreathèd smiles from him. But his very first words were to give her cause for a disquiet she didn't understand.

He said, 'I've called you for interview, Signorina Fleming, to give you the opportunity to explain to me some extra-mural actions and disloyalties to Plenair which could have the gravest possible consequences to your trusted position with us. You probably know to what I am referring?'

Aghast with dismay, Dinah stammered, 'I—I don't, I'm afraid, sir. You have me quite at a loss.'

He shrugged. 'Oh, come! I have consulted your contract, and I admit it contains nothing to bar you from undertaking some pin-money work in your spare time. So that if what you had been doing had been, say, some private typing or English coaching, that would be your affair. But this! This presumption on your privilege as an employee of Plenair to connive at a spy service directed at a selection of city hotels—certain of them on our own recommended list—happens to be very pointedly *our* affair. And now I hope you will not pretend you do not understand why I expect you to explain it, *signorina*?'

He waited through the silence Dinah needed to collect words for her defence. At last she said, 'I do understand that you think I am guilty of something of which I assure you, sir, I am not. I have accepted

160

no paid work outside my obligations to Plenair, and I've lent myself to no spy service. I was merely asked, in an entirely private capacity, to sample the services offered by those seven hotels you are referring to May I tell you, please, how it all came about?'

A frigid nod. 'Please do.'

'It was at a business dinner-party Signor Vidal gave to the members of the syndicate which was considering buying the chain of hotels in question——'

'And how did you come to be present at this business function?'

Dinah explained, 'You'll remember, sir, that I was burned out of my rented flat in the Calle Maser, and afterwards Signor Vidal, to whom I'd escorted two of his young cousins from England, offered me hospitality again until I found some other accommodation.'

'Very well. Go on.'

'And so, as I was living at the Palazzo d'Orio, I was occasionally asked to dinner with him and his friends, though more often I dined alone or went out for the evening. And it was partly because I was used to eating out alone in various restaurants that the suggestion was made that I should report on these places in which the syndicate was interested. They seemed to think,' Dinah added drily, 'that as I was a very ordinary lone female, my estimate of the treatment I got would be of some value to them.'

'A very amateur approach on their part, surely, and yours, a very minor contribution to their knowledge of the hotels?'

Dinah agreed, 'I thought so too. But it seems they

wanted a kind of worm's-eye view privately made
without any prejudice, and when they urged it on
me'—momentarily she was aware of a tiny nag
of memory of the scene—'I said I would do it and
make my report. And incidentally, if my experience
was a usual one, the two hotels of ours, the Orsini
and the Largo Vasto, emerged with flying colours. I
did make my reports in writing, I admit, and I did
turn them in to the syndicate. But I saw nothing in
what I did as being disloyal to the firm. After all, it
was only an amateur exercise, and the opinions I
expressed were only my own.'

'Some of which were adverse, no doubt?'

'One or two only. But when I thought the service
was poor, I admit I said so.'

'And what do you suppose our reputation would
be worth, if it got know in the city that a minor employee of ours was engaged in making secret paid
reports on independent establishments without their
agreement to be vetted so? Signor Vidal's syndicate
had every right to test for a sample of what they
were buying; they had no right whatsoever to pay you
extravagantly—you, employed by us—to do the
work for them. That, in my view, was double dealing
of the worst kind. I hope you agree?'

Dinah said tautly, 'I would—*if* there had been
any question of my being paid. But there was not.'

'You claim you did this survey for love—as one
might say? You received no pay at all?'

'I didn't want to. I didn't mean to. But in the end
I agreed I should have my bare expenses—for my
taxi, my meal and so on.'

'Amounting to, approximately?'

Dinah did a swift mental sum, arrived at a modest figure and named it.

Signor Corotti repeated it after her. 'And that is the total you have received?'

'Expect to receive. I haven't been paid it yet,' she corrected.

'But you say that is the total you claimed and should get?'

'I have only added it up in my head for you. But a few lire this way or that, yes.'

'Then how do you account for this?' He took a cheque from his desk drawer and flourished it. 'This is for a very different figure. In fact, deducting the odd amount which one supposes was for your expenses, it appears to show that you are to be paid around one hundred thousand lire for your visits to each of the seven hotels of your assignment—approximately seven hundred thousand lire in all. Well?'

Dinah felt all the blood drain from her face and downward, chilling her whole body. Her lips went dry and she had to moisten them before she could speak. 'That—that is astronomical, and completely absurd,' she said. 'May I examine the cheque? And may I ask how you came by it, Signor Corotti?'

'It has been temporarily entrusted to me by my informant on your activities, as I thought it only fair to confront you with it. But I have given my undertaking for its safe return.'

'And your informant?'

'I am sorry. The information was in confidence,

and I am not at liberty to name its source.'

Now Dinah's anger was rising, her confidence returning. 'The cheque, then? May I verify that?'

He passed it to her. The figures and wording were as he had said; the payee was herself and the cheque carried two signatures, one of them Betholde Lesogno, the other Cesare Vidal. Dinah fingered it for a moment, folded it once and across again, then tore it into pieces and allowed them to drop to the floor.

Signor Corotti stared. Dinah said, 'That's all that bit of nonsense is worth. But I daresay, if you ask your secretary to piece it together, your informant will accept it back. Meanwhile, it says nothing of me that is true, and it has no value, and I ask you to accept my word on that.'

He attempted to bluff it out. 'You only make a haughty gesture, *signorina*. A mere cheque could be written again.'

'I assure you, this cheque will *not* be written again. I never earned such money, nor had it offered to me for something I did voluntarily and in good faith and with no idea it might prejudice the interests of Plenair.'

'The cheque was made out to you for *some* purpose,' he maintained. 'However——' he hesitated, moved one or two things on his desk—'I only asked you here to get your explanation of the affair——'

'Which I have given you to the best of my ability.'

'By destroying the evidence of the cheque.'

'And by my word.'

Signor Corotti made a steeple of his fingers and

examined it dispassionately. 'Yes, well—I'm sure you will understand, *signorina*, that I have no choice but to suspend you until such time as——'

But Dinah, as sickened by his distrust as by what she read as Cesare's betrayal of her, had had enough. She stood up. 'And I,' she said, 'feel I have no choice but to ask you to accept my resignation from Plenair. To operate from now, if that's convenient. If not, from when it is.'

'I can make it convenient, *signorina*, if that's your wish.'

'Good,' said Dinah, driven by her pride, but not meaning 'Good' at all.

CHAPTER NINE

SHE went blindly back to the front office, her thoughts in a turmoil of anger, bewilderment and frustration.

Anger—how dared that man doubt her word and her good faith?

Bewilderment—why, *why* had Cesare let her believe the service he and his friends had asked of her had been voluntarily given, when he must have known that to pay her a ridiculously high fee for it while she was employed by Plenair was unethical by any business standards? She hated to think it of him. But he had signed that cheque, hadn't he? She had never seen Signor Lesogno's writing, but she knew Cesare's, and the signature had undoubtedly been his.

Frustration—today he was due to fly to Stockholm with his Swedish colleague, so that she hadn't even the bitter satisfaction of confronting him, hearing him try to justify his reasons and mincing no words in letting him know what she thought of them. As it was—she had a sense of stalemate which almost physically choked her.

She questioned whether she should confide in Trevor, ask his advice. But he was not at his desk. Etta said he was out, and was there any message Dinah would like to leave with her? Dinah said No, and again No, rather shortly when Etta asked eagerly whether at her interview with the manager he had asked her to stay on.

Arrived at her own desk, Dinah supposed that her ultimatum of 'Now' which Signor Corotti had accepted meant that she could leave at once. But she decided to see the day out. Tomorrow she would not come in and would have to see about booking her return journey to England.

And how she dreaded having to go back in such circumstances! Her people trusted her and would take her side. But the fact remained that she had had to resign to save herself probable dismissal, and their hopes of her prospects with Plenair had been as high as her own. She would almost certainly have left Venice before Cesare returned, but there was also the ordeal before her of explaining matters to his mother, and she could hardly expect any but divided loyalties from her. She would leave the Palazzo d'Orio under a cloud, if no worse, and whenever she had envisaged her parting from Cesare, she had meant it to be with dignity, however much her heart ached.

Between dealing with clients and inquiries and the telephone she sorted and tidied her desk, and listed details of tomorrow's work for the use of anyone who took her place. During the morning a clerk from Accountancy brought her a cheque for her pay to date and in lieu of notice, and she delivered the receipt herself to Signor Corotti's secretary. Her own immediate chief was on leave, so she had to explain herself to no one, and by tomorrow it would be common knowledge that she was not coming back.

She did not try to contact Trevor again, and when the office closed at seven she hurried away on foot. At least she would have the evening alone in which to lick her wounds, for she knew that Signora Vidal was dining out and would not be back until late.

She had little appetite for her dinner and went straight to her room after making a show of eating it. Mechanically she began her preparations for packing, her mind not on her task but ranging back and forward—back to her arrival with the twins and their frosty reception by Cesare; to the camaraderie they had achieved with him, while her own relationship remained rather fraught, always warmed by his praise and chilled by his indifference—and forward to a future that was going to be empty of him for good.

Looking through the books she had acquired since she came to Venice, she remembered she had left one, a collection of coloured plates of the Doges' Palace paintings, in the *salotto*. She went down to fetch it and had just taken it from a side table when the door opened and someone—Cesare—came in.

He threw his briefcase on a chair. '*Ciao*,' he greeted her. 'You wouldn't expect to see me?'

Temporarily both her wits and her pent-up anger against him deserted her. 'Of course not. You—you're in Stockholm,' she said foolishly.

'Am I? So much for plans! There was a lightning strike of staff at the airport, and after waiting all day to fly out, there's no hope now until further notice. Tomorrow—perhaps, though more likely not. Have you had dinner?' he asked.

168

'Ye-es.'

'Well, I haven't, and I'm starving.'

'I—I'll tell Tomasa. Or does she know you are back?'

'No. But here's a better idea. Will you come out with me for a meal somewhere?'

Her rancour flooded back. 'I've told you, I have eaten. So no, thank you.'

His brows lifted. ' "No, thank you"—just like that? How extremely glacial! I'd have thought you could at least watch me eat and join me in coffee and a liqueur?'

'Well, I couldn't. It would choke me.' She had braced herself for attack. 'What's more, I'm surprised you dare to ask me—in the circumstances.'

He stared. 'Dare to ask you to dine? What do you mean? In what circumstances?'

'You must know. Or did you think you could get away with tricking me into doing a job for you that I believed was just a—a goodwill thing that I was glad to do, as long as it was voluntary and amateur and couldn't prejudice my position at Plenair at all?'

She watched him work it out. 'You're talking about the survey you did for us? But you did do it voluntarily, though I'd remind you you agreed to accept your expenses,' he said.

'My expenses, yes, though I didn't expect even them. You had made it sound so casual—all of you had—that I never suspected you had it in mind to try to—either bribe me or insult me with the ridiculous figure on that cheque. Not to mention that you must have known I couldn't take any direct payment

169

for any job while I was employed by Plenair and without their permission. Especially one which involved reporting on hotels in which the firm had interests.'

'If we had thought about it, of course we should have known. But this cheque—the one I signed before I left for Stockholm and gave to Bertholde Lesogno to complete and sign it himself in the name of the syndicate, and then to pass it to you?'

'*That* cheque, yes.'

'But what about it? It only covered your expenses!'

'Expenses? *Expenses?*' she echoed. 'At seven hundred thousand lire plus? Nearly seventy English pounds for each hotel I visited? Expenses indeed!'

'Oh, nonsense,' he scorned. 'You were seeing double when you read it. Where is it, anyway? Show it to me.'

'I can't. I tore it up. And your friend Lesogno didn't send it to me. It came into the hands of the Plenair manager, Signor Corotti, and as he concluded, or had been told, that it was pay for something I shouldn't have been doing for money, he felt justified in dismissing me. And if he couldn't believe me, perhaps he was.'

'He dismissed you, without hearing your side?'

'He would have done, but I forestalled him. I resigned myself.'

'But how did he come by the cheque?'

'From a ''source'' he wouldn't name to me.'

'Lesogno?'

'How should I know? Signor Corotti had undertaken to return it when he had faced me with it, but I destroyed it in front of him.'

'Of course.'

'But he said I was only making a gesture; probably because he had frightened me into repudiating it. That I knew it could be written again, was his conclusion. I could tell he didn't believe a word I was saying.'

Cesare said tautly, 'He'll believe it—or else—when I get next to him!'

'You?' There was a world of disillusion in Dinah's tone. 'You signed the cheque!'

'I've told you,' he retorted, 'I signed it blank. Which means that some time between then and when it was slipped to your manager, this absurd figure was entered on it, and friend Lesogno is going to have to explain *that*!'

Dinah was silent. Something strange and disconcerting had happened. From the enemy whom she had thought she must force to defend himself, Cesare had suddenly turned ally, on the defensive for her. There was a cliché for that—something about the spiking of guns—— Now she heard him saying, 'But first of all, we'll interview this Corotti and make him name his informant. Where can he be reached at this hour?'

'Only at his home. The office is closed.'

'Then his home it shall be. His number will be in the book?'

But Dinah suddenly snapped, 'No! No, leave it. I fought my battle with him and I'm not involving you in another. Whoever gave him the cheque only did it to get me into trouble with Plenair. Which it did, and

I'm disgraced there, and I couldn't—wouldn't go back, whatever mud you stir up.'

Cesare came slowly across the room to where she stood, the big book, the purpose of her errand to the *salotto*, clasped in front of her like an armoured breastplate. Standing close over her, he said, 'You are not serious. The mud has to be stirred. Because you're not alone in this. Your character has been called into question, and you won't get another job in the same line until the thing has been cleared up. Besides, Lesogno's and my good faith are in doubt. No, Dinah, you can't fight it alone, nor 'leave it'. It's out of your hands.'

'But I *have* fought it alone! It's finished.'

He shook his head. 'No. Someone has done this to embarrass you and worse—even to costing you your job, which is probably what was intended; so that if you leave it here, they have succeeded. You have made an enemy of someone, girl—don't you realise that? How the thing was managed, one can't know, but I'm not going to rest until I find out. I'm going straight to the telephone now.'

Still holding the book with one hand, she caught at his wrist with the other as he turned. 'No, Cesare, please!' she begged. 'I mean it.'

He turned back. 'Why?'

She fumbled for a reason—not the true one— which he might accept. 'Because,' she said, 'I thought you were responsible, and now you've proved to me that you weren't, I—well, I haven't the right to try to lean on you, to expect you to help.'

Thought up on the spur of her need to give him a

reason, it was a lame effort, she knew. But for a long moment he seemed to consider its validity before he said quietly and tensely, 'Then we must give you the right, mustn't we? Dinah, will you marry me?'

Wide-eyed and in silence, she stared at him. The question made no sense, for, spoken from him to her, the words had no meaning. Fleetingly she wondered what it was about her which did not inspire love, but which had prompted two men to offer her marriage in a reckless impulse to protect her from her world.

For this was a *déja-vu* scene—a re-lived one, one that had enacted before. In a rash moment Trevor had asked her to marry him in order to guard her from scandal, and now Cesare, even if he were only momentarily serious, was doing the same. But of course he wasn't serious; he couldn't be, and the thought that he could suppose the empty offer would comfort or reassure her was a wound which struck deep. As she remembered telling Trevor—if marriage had been for them, they would not have had to argue the pros and cons of it; they would have been in each other's arms. And if any warmth or tenderness, rather than quixotry, had inspired Cesare's question, she would have known, *known* before now that he felt for her more than the lightweight friendship they had lately attained. There would have been an awareness, a response to her feeling for him. And he had allowed her none.

At last she muttered, her voice thick, 'That was pretty unfair, wasn't it?'

His dark eyes sparked. 'Unfair to you? What do you mean?'

173

'Unworthy of yourself, then. If it wasn't meant flippantly as a joke, then it was callous, and that's something I've never known you to be.'

'Thank you.' A muscle twitched at the corner of his mouth. 'It's something, I suppose, that I'm not a monster of insentience. So it had to be a joke, had it?'

'Of course. What else? And I'm afraid I didn't find it funny——' But there Dinah had had enough. She could not go bandying mere words with him, arguing the unarguable, fearing to reveal to him the depth of her hurt. She had to escape.

She backed a step, turned and left him, not looking back, not expecting him to follow or to stop her, which he did not. In the hall, in a mechanical reflex she did not later remember making, she picked up her bag from a table where she had left it when coming in earlier, and went out by the front door, letting it close heavily behind her.

For a minute or two she stood irresolutely on the quay, then began to walk, unaware of any decision to go either right or left, but only of her need to put distance between herself and the Palazzo d'Orio—and Cesare.

It was always easy, in Venice, to walk without purpose or direction. A wide paved *calle*, lined with shops, would offer itself; a shadowed *riva* would branch off; a hump-backed bridge would invite; a mere passage between walls would give on to a broad *campo*, its expanse peopled by groups of teenagers, children on tricycles and romping dogs.

Dinah wandered aimlessly, trying to forget humiliation and chagrin and the cruel injustice from which Cesare had pretended it was his duty to rescue her.

She must go back some time; she owed his mother gratitude and explanations as to her imminent departure from Venice and the Palazzo's hospitality. So somehow she must walk off anger and despair until she could return with dignity and control. And perhaps, if Cesare were able to leave for Sweden tomorrow, she need not see him again.

But it was difficult to keep her mind from churning, from remembering. Now she was recalling the flash of insight she had experienced when she had told Signor Corotti of how she had been urged into doing her amateur survey. For who, among the people at that dinner-party, had been the most subtle in persuading Cesare and the others that she, Dinah, was the ideal person for the job? That had been Francia Lagna! For some, perhaps then undefined purpose of Francia's own, she had *wanted* to involve Dinah, had seen advantage to herself in it, however vaguely. But ultimately there had been nothing vague about the revenge she had achieved. For as soon as Cesare had mentioned her 'enemy', Dinah had realised that without doubt she had one, and who it was who could have sought to injure her so cruelly. Yet because the Princess was so close to Cesare, Dinah could not name her, and so had had to resort to the feeble reason she had given for insisting that he should not interfere. And look where that had led! Straight to that spurious suggestion that it was his duty to marry her. But there she was, back again full circle to bitterness and questioning and regret. She must, she *would* think about something else—about the twins, about going home and being welcomed there, about Trevor and Etta being happy—anything.

It had been a heavy day of brooding cloud, and the light was fading when she found her wandering had brought her near to the Calle Maser and she remembered she had promised Maria Pacelli that she would keep an eye on the progress of the repairs to the apartment building after the fire. When she had made the promise the errand hadn't seemed urgent, but now that she would be leaving Venice as soon as she could arrange it, she decided to look at the place this evening. Doing so would 'take her mind off' . . .

She went through the archway into the courtyard. The builders had knocked off work for the day, but she could see that the gutted two lower floors had reached an encouraging state of repair, though they were not yet reoccupied. The entrance door from the court had always stood open, as it did now, and remembering that the key to Maria Pacelli's flat was in her bag, Dinah went up the stairs to it.

As she knew, the fire had not reached their floor, but earlier she had arranged for most of the furnishings to go into store, leaving behind only some kitchen equipment in locked cupboards and the fixtures. She opened on to a dust-begrimed scene which would not be habitable again until it had been fully redecorated. The rooms were so dark behind their shutters that she had to throw them back, and as she did so the first of the rain which had been threatening all day began to fall, and in the distance thunder growled.

There was little to be done about the rooms' griminess; the builders' traffic in the courtyard and the dust of their demolition would make it just as bad tomorrow, she knew. But in pity and regret for how the place had looked after Cesare's furbishing of it for her, she found a duster and a window-cloth and gave it such cleaning as she could while she waited for the rain to give over. She had brought no coat when she had fled from the Palazzo, and in minutes her light dress and sandals would be soaked through.

But the rain did not give over. It increased and came down with steady persistence—the thorough-going, flood-causing rain of the sub-tropical equinox, the kind of rain which, at the change of season, the Venetian plain knew well and which could empty the city streets of their night life and the canals of their craft with the seeming legerdemain of a conjuring trick, yet which tomorrow might usher in a cloudless dawn and another sun-drenched day.

Dinah had to draw the shutters close against its drive, and sit in the increasing dark while she waited to be able to leave. Nobody was going to come home to this shell of a building; no light nor heat was connected, and, lacking a chair, all she could do was to prop herself on the padded windowseat in the bedroom where in happier days she had often spent the twilight of summer evenings looking out over the roofs and chimneys and television aerials of the city until the real dark came down.

Now it was intensely dark and the rain still drummed. She supposed she must soon make a dash for it, but not quite yet. For it wasn't only the rain which deterred her; she dreaded her return to the Palazzo more. So she would wait a little while longer . . . not too long . . . . perhaps another ten minutes or so . . .

She woke with a start, blinking and shaking her head in wonder. How could she have slept, with her mind in such a turmoil and her body in such a cramped, half-sitting, half-lying position? She remembered now having shut her eyes briefly, thinking that if sleep would come—which it wouldn't—it would be a welcome respite from her troubles. But it had come. For how long? She had no torch with which to look at her watch, but if she waited and were lucky, one of the many church clocks of the city would signal the hour to her. Surely it couldn't be very late?

She listened for the rain. It had eased slightly, but it was still coming down. And then the deep tongue of San Pedro's clock spoke—boom, boom, boom. Three strokes only, then silence. Three o'clock in the morning! How could she creep back to the Palazzo at such an hour?

She stood up stiffly, then walked about the empty room. What would they think of her? Where would they suppose she was?

Guilt was now added to all the rest. Rain or no rain, she should have gone back at some reasonable time; she had no right to have put Cesare's mother to the worry she knew she would suffer for her. Cesare would have told her how she had flung out of the house without a coat and, as far as they knew, without money for a hotel room. But though she debated going back straight away, she thought it best to wait until first light when she knew Tomasa would be up and about, and she could hope that the Signora and Cesare were, mercifully, still in bed.

It was cold now, and she groped into a cupboard where she thought she had left a couple of blankets. She had, and wrapped herself in them and went back to the window-seat to wait for morning. It was a very long time until the sky began to pale, then turned saffron-yellow as the sun climbed, though the court-yard would be in shadow for some hours yet. The houses round about came to life; shutters were thrown back, housewives shouted *Buon giorno* to each other across the court and the inevitable Venetian pigeons fluttered and strutted in the hope of a meal. It was time for Dinah to go.

She put away the blankets, wiped her hands and face with her handkerchief and ran her pocket-comb through her hair. But as she paused for a last look round, there was a tread on the stairs. Someone was coming up them, up to this floor. She went through to the vestibule and waited, then opened the door to come face to face with—Cesare's mother!

Dinah was speechless. The Signora, panting a little, said, 'Well, well! Put two and two together, and what do they make? Aren't you going to ask me in, child?'

There was kindliness about that 'child', and Dinah, disarmed and contrite, found her tongue in a babble.

'Yes, of course.' She stood aside and the Signora swept through into the living-room. 'I—I'm so sorry. I didn't mean—— It was the storm. I know I ought to have braved it, but I—sort of fell asleep, and——'

The Signora was looking round the empty room.

'Fell asleep? Standing up? Like a horse?' she inquired.

'No. There's a window-seat in the bedroom.'

'Then lead me to it. Those stairs——!' In the bedroom she approved the window-seat, 'H'm, better than nothing,' sat down on it and invited Dinah to sit beside her.

'Well, now——' she began.

Dinah said, 'I can't think how you found me, *signora*.'

'And you'd like me to say "Simple"? Well, it wasn't. I didn't get home until midnight, and by then Cesare had telephoned the police and the hospitals and every hotel he thought you knew. After a couple of hours he insisted on my going to bed, but he stayed up, and it wasn't until half an hour ago that he waked me to tell me that Tomasa had come up with a clue.'

'Tomasa?' said Dinah puzzled.

'It seems that you had mentioned to her that you had promised that girl you had exchanged with you would make time to see how the repairs to this place were going on.' The Signora paused. 'In the circumstances, Cesare thought it an odd time for you to choose to do it, but I persuaded him it was worth our looking.'

'In the circumstances?' questioned Dinah faintly.

'Of how you ran out on him. He said he thought it unlikely you did that in any mood for making a cold-blooded survey of property.'

'Yes, well—I walked and walked. I had to. And when I found myself near here, I thought I might as well come in. That was before the rain began. You—you know what had happened before I ran away?'

180

'I do. And that before he got alarmed as to your whereabouts, Cesare had sorted the whole thing out. He telephoned Bertholde Lesogno, your chief, and then the Villa Bacardi, of course.'

'The Villa Barcadi?' The name had meaning for Dinah.

'Yes. Francia Lagna hadn't been able to get to Stockholm either. She was still at the Villa and Cesare spoke to her.'

'O-oh,' murmured Dinah on a long-drawn breath.

The Signora said briskly, 'I see you understand how the woman was involved. Had you guessed it for yourself? And when?'

'Not—not how. And not until Cesare suggested I must have an enemy. Then I think I almost knew, because I knew she had never liked me. But I couldn't think how she managed it, and I still can't.'

'And I'll leave Cesare to enlighten you on the details.'

'Oh—do I have to see him? He is not here with you?'

'How do you suppose I got here at this hour, if he didn't bring me in the launch?' his mother countered. 'But tell me, child, when you suspected La Lagna, why didn't you say so to Cesare?'

'Because—I felt I mustn't accuse her to him. It wouldn't have been fair, considering what they were —are—to each other. And when Cesare—well, when he——' Dinah broke off, her lips out of control. 'Well, did he tell you that when he saw how distressed and worried I was, out of some quirk of pity for me he *proposed* to me? Not meaning it, of course.

How could he? And I couldn't take any more. So I ran——'

The Signora said calmly and distinctly, 'He told me, yes, that he asked you to marry him, meaning every word.'

'But he couldn't! It was a joke or misplaced kindness or—something. He knew he would have to take it back. He doesn't love me!'

'Any more than you love him?'

Dinah looked out over the chimneypots and the aerials, and for the second time in hours said, 'That's unfair.'

'Which gives me my answer, and I have suspected it for some time. Why else do you suppose I catechized you about Cesare and Francia Lagna if I didn't want to find out what your reaction was? So you have fallen in love with my bad son?'

Dinah could only nod. 'I shall get over it,' she muttered after a moment.

'Will you indeed? That doesn't speak too well for your future with him!'

'My future?'

'Tch, weren't you listening, child? He asked you to marry him because he wants to marry you. Haven't I made that plain?'

'You mean—he has said so?'

'If he hadn't, I should still have guessed. Mothers have intuitions about these things.' The Signora rose and made a fastidious gesture of brushing down her skirt after a critical glance at the padding of the window bench. 'Not exactly an ideal loveseat,' she commented of it,' but I daresay you will manage. I'm going to send Cesare to you now.'

182

'Why, where is he?'

'Below. I told him to give me ten minutes with you, and my time is up. I'll see myself out. In a two-by-four place like this, who couldn't?'

'Oh, please, I——' Dinah begged in panic.

Signor Vidal turned back on her way to the door. 'Shy? Scared? Not looking your best, h'm? What of it? In marriage there will be plenty of times when you won't be, or he won't be looking his. Dirty faces and unshaven chins and colds in the head are great levellers, but you'll love each other all the same, if you begin that way. Cesare's father and I did, so believe me, I *know*.'

For Dinah there was a heart-thumping, sense-benumbing pause before she heard Cesare coming up the stairs. Then he was there, holding out both hands to her—real, virile and very, very dear. But *hers*?

His fingers were beckoning an invitation to her, and when she put her hands in his, he drew her close.

Over the top of her head he asked, 'Why did you run away? Or no—Mamma has told me why you thought you had to—because you couldn't believe I was serious. But, *carissima*, would any man commit himself so far without a serious purpose to it? Now would he?'

'Trevor Land did—in words,' Dinah murmured.

'For duty's sake to you, though he didn't love you? But why should you think *I* could hurt you in the same way?'

'But Trevor didn't hurt me. I had never loved him enough for that, and I knew it before he did.'

Cesare held her off and looked accusingly into her eyes. 'You let me think you were hurt, and that it

183

was out of pride that you turned him down!'

'My letting you think so wasn't deliberate, though I realised later that you did.'

'Then why didn't you put me right?'

'I didn't suppose it was enough concern to you.'

'No concern? Why, by the time you had edged your way into my heart—and that had happened long since—my nerves jumped with jealousy at every sight or mention of the man! And when I thought he had jilted you, I was ready to go berserk. *And* crazy to comfort you, though I judged you were in no mood for being consoled just then. And anyway, what of the little dogmatist who claimed a woman would always know when she was loved, and yet didn't know about *me*?'

'I thought I should know,' she admitted. 'I hoped you liked me, but if you did, it would only be because you said I debated like a man, and I made you fight to win an argument.'

He nodded. 'I remember the occasion. Yet nothing else I said—or did—that night told you otherwise, and more?'

She looked down, unable to meet his searching eyes.

'I'd wanted you—so badly—to kiss me——'

'Well, didn't I? With feeling which you should have understood!'

'But afterwards you said there was no future in it,'

'I was only making it easy for you to retreat in good order.'

'But I didn't *want* to retreat!'

'So I'd hoped—while you seemed all acquiescent

and your lips were warm and liquid under mine. But as soon as I let you go, you were as distant as if I had never touched you. Why?'

'Princess Lagna,' Dinah said, leaving the name to explain itself.

'Francia? You didn't understand she was a business asset I was cultivating and sponsoring for our mutual benefit? Which she will justify in time, though not now where I'm concerned. I've finished with her. But you thought marriage to her was a clause in our contract? No—really!'

'You were always together, and people said so.'

'People?'

'Well, Signora Rienzi, and Trevor told me it was the general gossip. The twins, who didn't like the Princess, had the same idea, and even your mother——'

Cesare threw back his head and laughed. 'She frightened you too, did she?'

'Frightened me?'

'At my request, sweetheart. On her own, she had guessed what I felt about you, and did what she could to help. For instance, her diplomatic headache, the night she sent us to the Casa La Corba without her, though it was her homecoming we were supposed to be celebrating. And when I admitted it, and suggested she might test your reaction to her pretended fear I was going to marry Francia, she played up nobly. You *were* frightened, and showed it, she said.'

Dinah thought back to the signora's hints and questions on the day they had spent at Le Rose. Her hands on Cesare's arms administered a mock-threatening shake. 'Oh—you!' She had time to accuse him

185

before he gathered her close again, making of the hard pressure of his body and his demand for her lips a claim which she could not, and knew she never would, deny.

Passion surged, spoke and promised, and on the promise, was at last content with mere tenderness. Hands gently explored. A finger smoothed an eyebrow. Lips found the hollow of a throat. Tongues murmured lovers' foolish nothings. They were confident of future enchantment in store, and tenderness was enough.

Then they were talking again, telling, questioning, answering.

'What did you mean, when you said you had finished with the Princess?' Dinah asked, hoping she knew.

'Just that, and she knows it. And why. But how much did Mamma tell you about her murky little plot against you?'

'Only that she was involved in my—trouble. Which, when I thought about it, I had more or less guessed.'

'Though not guessing that she did it for fear of my interest in you? She claimed she only did it for a joke—to give you some minor difficulty with your chief. Want to hear how she did it?'

'Please. Though then I want to forget it.'

'And you shall. It began with Francia's dropping in at Bertholde's office to leave a message for Signora Lesogno. While she was there he was called away, he says, and when he came back, the cheque for you which he had signed but hadn't filled in, wasn't still on his desk. He thought no more of it when he couldn't find it, knowing that if he had inadvertently destroyed it, it could be made out again. Once I knew this, I made Francia confess she had filched it, though with only some vague idea of using it against you. When she realised how she could, she filled it in for that absurd sum which looked like bribery, and took it to your chief, leaving him to draw his conclusions. She knew the trick couldn't hold credence for long. But while it did, she saw it as—fun.'

'*Fun?*' Dinah echoed faintly.

'Exactly.' Cesare compressed his lips. 'So then I rang your chief; said a few trenchant things to him, made him promise you a full apology, and told him you wouldn't be going back to Plenair.'

'I could. If he apologises, perhaps I ought to,' Dinah hesitated.

'As a married woman? Over my dead body!' Cesare declared.

'Oh——!'

'Oh!' he mimicked. 'Hadn't you realised that is what you will be, just as soon as I can arrange it?'

'You haven't asked me to m——' She checked and blushed. 'Oh, but you did!'

'And once is enough, if it gets the right answer. And you've given it since, haven't you, my love, my love? So come here again, before we go down to Mamma to tell her that history has repeated itself with another Italian–English alliance in the family.'

In his arms once more, Dinah asked, 'Will she be

pleased? Does she like me enough? Did she really want it to happen for us?'

Cesare said, 'If I know Mamma it will not be long before she is claiming that she planned the whole thing. You'll see.'

They found the Signora sunning herself in the launch and engaged on a small piece of *petit-point*.

'I always take to my embroidery in moments of crisis,' she explained as she put it way. 'Well?'

Cesare helped Dinah into her seat and stooped to kiss his mother before taking his place at the wheel. 'The lady is mine, Mamma. All is well,' he told her. 'No crisis. No call for you to be plying your needle at all.'

'Good.' His mother's smile for Dinah was sweet and welcoming. 'Then as soon as we get home I must send a telegram. Two telegrams. One to Reading and one to Oxford——'

There was a moment's silence. Then—'To the twins?' Cesare queried. 'Telling them what, if one may venture to ask, *mamma mia*?'

'Saying the same to both of them. "Mission accomplished. They will be married at Christmas, and you must be here." When I was in England, we discussed both the possibility and the desirability of getting you two together, and obviously I have to let them know how well we have succeeded, haven't I?'

Cesare echoed gravely, 'But obviously,' then sent a sly, knowing grin at Dinah.

'What did I tell you?' he said.

But if the Signora heard or understood, she gave no sign.

Did you miss any of these exciting Harlequin Omnibus 3-in-1 volumes?

Anne Hampson

Essie Summers

Margaret Way

Margaret Malcolm

Eleanor Farnes

Kay Thorpe

18 magnificent Omnibus volumes to choose from:

 *Betty Neels*

Betty Neels #3
Tangled Autumn (#1569)
Wish with the Candles (#1593)
Victory for Victoria (#1625)

Violet Winspear

Violet Winspear #5
Raintree Valley (#1555)
Black Douglas (#1580)
The Pagan Island (#1616)

Anne Hampson

Anne Hampson #4
Isle of the Rainbows (#1646)
The Rebel Bride (#1672)
The Plantation Boss (#1678)

Margery Hilton

Margery Hilton
The Whispering Grove (#1501)
Dear Conquistador (#1610)
Frail Sanctuary (#1670)

Rachel Lindsay

Rachel Lindsay
Love and Lucy Granger (#1614)
Moonlight and Magic (#1648)
A Question of Marriage (#1667)

Jane Arbor

Jane Arbor #2
The Feathered Shaft (#1443)
Wildfire Quest (#1582)
The Flower on the Rock (#1665)

Great value in reading at $2.25 per volume

Joyce Dingwell #3
Red Ginger Blossom (#1633)
Wife to Sim (#1657)
The Pool of Pink Lilies (#1688)

Hilary Wilde
The Golden Maze (#1624)
The Fire of Life (#1642)
The Impossible Dream (#1685)

Flora Kidd

Flora Kidd
If Love Be Love (#1640)
The Cave of the White Rose (#1663)
The Taming of Lisa (#1684)

Lucy Gillen

Lucy Gillen #2
Sweet Kate (#1649)
A Time Remembered (#1669)
Dangerous Stranger (#1683)

Gloria Bevan

Gloria Bevan
Beyond the Ranges (#1459)
Vineyard in a Valley (#1608)
The Frost and the Fire (#1682)

Jane Donnelly

Jane Donnelly
The Mill in the Meadow (#1592)
A Stranger Came (#1660)
The Long Shadow (#1681)

Complete and mail this coupon today!

A Growing Moon

by JANE ARBOR

Cesare Vidal's attitude left Dinah silently fuming. He'd shifted responsibility for the twins to her shoulders and apparently had no interest in them—even though they were his cousins.

Maybe she should have been flattered, but she would have gladly exchanged his airy confidence in her for a little old-fashioned male concern. Why couldn't she be given a trace of the solicitude he showed for Princess Francia Lagna?

 Harlequin Romances

Your passports to a dream—eight new, heartwarming and exciting romantic novels, never before published, are available every month wherever paperbacks are sold.

02108